A Candlelight Ecstasy Romance®

SHE WOULD DENY HERSELF NOTHING.
NOT THAT DAY....

Ronnie tilted her head back, her eyes shining. Her fingers caressed the rich thickness of his black hair, touching it with devouring reverence. His eyes began to smolder once more as they bored into hers, still carrying that infinite tenderness. His lips touched hers softly. These things she savored sweetly for a cherishable moment, her mouth pliant, her lips moistly parted. Then a brushfire began—a longing, a yearning, a needing of such intensity, it stole her breath away. It took her from the confines of the cabin to a haven where sight, sound, and reality were all lost in abandon to one overwhelming sensation—*him.*

A CANDLELIGHT ECSTASY ROMANCE ®

A SEASON
FOR LOVE

Heather Graham

A CANDLELIGHT ECSTASY ROMANCE ®

Published by
Dell Publishing Co., Inc.
1 Dag Hammarskjold Plaza
New York, New York 10017

Dell ® TM 681510, Dell Publishing Co., Inc.

Candlelight Ecstasy Romance®, 1,203,540, is a registered
trademark of Dell Publishing Co., Inc.,
New York, New York.

ISBN: 0–440–18041–4

Printed in the United States of America
First printing—July 1983

For Dennis

To Our Readers:

We have been delighted with your enthusiastic response to Candlelight Ecstasy Romances®, and we thank you for the interest you have shown in this exciting series.

In the upcoming months we will continue to present the distinctive sensuous love stories you have come to expect only from Ecstasy. We look forward to bringing you many more books from your favorite authors, and also the very finest work from new authors of contemporary romantic fiction.

As always, we are striving to present the unique, absorbing love stories that you enjoy most—books that are more than ordinary romance.

Your suggestions and comments are always welcome. Please write to us at the address below.

Sincerely,

The Editors
Candlelight Romances
1 Dag Hammarskjold Plaza
New York, New York 10017

PROLOGUE

Tears filled her eyes as she left the house.

She had contained and concealed them through the preceding argument, but now, as she faced the wind, she could allow them to form.

Now that she was alone.

Which was funny really, because she was always alone.

Always calm, always staid, always perfect . . .

Always alone, even among others, even with the man for whom she shed her tears. They spoke, but they never talked. Circumstances barred intimacy, bitterness barred friendship. All she received was harshness.

But she understood, and it was terrible to understand. It meant becoming the marble she lived with, never really showing emotion, choosing a course and following it, humoring him. . . .

She was humoring him now by leaving the house and taking to the sea, a vision of his limpid blue eyes in her mind. Eyes she understood, and fought against.

Standing on deck surrounded by people, her tears left her own sapphire gaze, and it became frosty, assessing. Completely confident, she entered the world she had no wish to join. Humoring. . . .

Suddenly, like the closing of one's eyes after a camera flash, a new vision replaced that of the pale blue eyes—a pair of eyes so darkly, vividly brown that they burned with a coal fire.

She blinked, realizing that she had just seen such a pair of eyes.

And to her dismay that quickly flashed image stayed with her, haunting her. She focused on pale, powdery blue, but the lighter color became continually obliterated by the darker hue.

Extraordinary, really.

And very, very foolish.

Because she would also leave the sea and return to the house.

CHAPTER ONE

Statuesque.

It was the only word to adequately describe the sleek beauty of the tall brunette. Although a multitude of attractive young women frolicked around the poolside, displaying varying amounts of curvaceous flesh, she alone had the power to rivet the eye. She wasn't as voluptuous as some, nor was the teal-blue bikini she wore as bare as many others.

What attracted the eye went further than the perfectly proportioned build and smooth, golden-tanned skin. It was in the grace of her slightest movement, in the fluidity of her composed walk, in the very poise and serenity with which she surveyed the scene she had come upon.

She was as stunning and lithe as a panther, mused one of the men who watched her, and the thought struck him that, like the discreetly moving panther, she was seeking prey with slow, confident deliberation.

He almost laughed aloud at his own thought. With the flick of a finger, this one could draw the male of the species to her without ever needing to seek anything. He could easily imagine half the men around him swarming to her feet on their knees, as if she were a queen bee.

He sat back comfortably in the lounge chair, unaware that he was her male counterpart, and that the majority of the females taking the three-day cruise—from the giggling teenagers to the graying, plump matrons—had already created romantic fantasies in their minds with him in the starring role.

Drake O'Hara was the perfect picture of man at his very best. Black Irish, they would have called him in the land of his fore-bears, and like the Spaniards of the lost Armada who had been wrecked upon the Emerald Isle, he was dark, his hair a shade deeper than india ink, his eyes a deep, arresting brown. His complexion tanned easily to a golden copper, and when he smiled—an act that could be charming or chilling, depending on his motive—his straight white teeth were almost startling against the backdrop of his skin and the neat black mustache that framed lips that could either be full and sensuous or grim and tight. He had inherited his coloring from the Spaniards, his fiery temper from the Irish. Fortunately, he was also capable of learned control and diplomacy, traits he liked to think he inherited from his American mother.

Drake was giving no thoughts to his own ancestry at the moment. Beneath the shadow of misty glasses, his dark eyes were fixed contemplatively on the brunette. Her poise, he decided, was helped along by her bone structure. Her face was an exquisite oval, the cheekbones high, the hollows classic, the eyes—set beneath slender arched brows—large, thick-lashed, and almost shockingly blue. Her classic nose fit her classic face—small and aquiline. Only her lips offset the marble coolness of her untouchable beauty; they were too full for severity, too sensuously shaped for innocence.

Yet the chin beneath them was determined, and on second speculation, those magnificent blue eyes were hard crystal gems. Hmmm . . . hard, but something else. If she didn't seem such a bastion of icy reserve, Drake mused, he would think of that something else as—tragic.

It was with a bit of surprise that Drake realized she was returning his assessing surveillance. Well aware that she knew he watched her, he made no attempt to avert his eyes. Nor did she. He knew too that she studied him with the same thoroughness to which he had subjected her.

What he didn't know was that she watched him with a wrenching pain. Long ago, in a different lifetime, she had loved a man as magnificent as he. A man of indomitable strength, of pride and arrogance that were uniquely gifts of birth. Broad in the shoulders and chest, ruggedly trim in the hips and legs; tightly sinewed, muscle-coiled rather than muscle-bound . . .

Long, long, ago, so agonizingly long ago, such a man had been hers by right. Now nothing could be right again.

But she knew the message in his eyes, and although the inadvertent action was imperceptible, she swallowed convulsively. Far from seeking prey as he had whimsically envisioned, she was staunchly set on not becoming prey. She didn't want to form any associations, not even the most innocently casual ones. She didn't even want to be on this three-day cruise. For the briefest second she blinked, and caught the mist of tears that threatened to obscure her vision.

If only . . .

God, she wondered fleetingly, why had she seen him? Her resolve had been fixed, her soul could bear no more scars.

But she had seen him, and he was touching her, with his eyes only, as no other man had or could, no, not even Jamie, all those years before. . . .

He lifted a hand to remove his sunglasses. Dimly she noted that hand, shivering within. It was long and broad, and flecked with a smattering of crisp black curls. His fingers were long, the nails short and clipped neatly. She could almost feel the rugged touch of his hands, and a moment of dizziness and fear overwhelmed her. Fear of him, fear of herself. She so desperately longed to just talk to him that she was beginning to rationalize, her mind and senses in a devastating tug of war. She couldn't, she couldn't. . . . But, dear God, why not? She would never see him again . . . this was a ship, and it would dock, and the passengers would go their separate ways. She closed her eyes tightly for the flicker of an instant, waging a fierce battle with the conscience that ruled her. Talk, perhaps share a drink. Was it so very wrong of her, just this once, to envision the simple pleasure of a man's conversation . . . his masculine touch?

13

Oh, God. . . .

She couldn't help herself thinking. Her poise, her manner, her appearance . . . all these she could control. But dreams swept heedlessly into her mind, there was no blocking them. They could tear down the defenses of the strongest willpower.

His black eyes were piercingly upon her as he rose from the lounge chair. She was tall, but she could see immediately that he would tower above her. His legs—adorned with the same masculine curls as his hands and chest—were very long. Added to the impressive length of his tapered torso, they made him very tall indeed, imposingly tall. . . .

He watched her as he walked, his strides long, assured—natural. The easy walk of a confident man. It was not her he approached, but the crystal water that separated them.

He would never need to impose himself; his invitation was out. Acceptance was up to her.

He plunged into the ship's small saltwater pool in a manner she should have anticipated—a perfect, clear-cut dive.

This was it. The messages they had been sending through eye contact were now being tested. He had taken the first move—a relief to her. But now she had to take the second.

Now or never.

Not a muscle in her face twitched. Intense immersion into the drama of life had given her the composure that went far beyond her years.

But inside, it seemed as if her very blood froze. Yearning tinged by guilt waged a war with fear.

And the guilt was ridiculous. She was trying to fulfill a dying man's plea.

But still it was there, because of the yearning. Because she wanted to feel again . . . because she wanted so desperately to know happiness, if only for stolen moments, if only superficially.

The seconds were ticking by. . . .

Drake emerged at the shallow end of the small pool just in time to see her exquisitely sculpted, alabaster-sleek body cut into the water as cleanly as his had. And again he was reminded of the sultry beauty of a feline. But, he wondered, in a quick flight of Gaelic fancy, what was the nature of this cat he counter-stalked. Was she a tigress with claws, or a domesticated, purring Persian?

It didn't really matter. She had completely intrigued him. He had always been fond of and had a way with the fairer sex; he knew their games and played them confidently by the rules. A certain gallantry stayed with him from a bygone age—he only played with those who also knew the rules.

What was her game, he wondered idly. Did she want to be wined and dined and danced? Flattered and cajoled?

There was of course the possibility that she knew who he was and that money or prestige had been the draw. He was self-confident, assured, and, admittedly, arrogant at times, but he had never deluded himself that he had always been sought for his charm alone. Many a fair damsel who had come his way had actually worn the tarnished glitter of gold in her eye . . . and a hope that a band of the same color upon her finger would be the reward.

Drake wasn't really a cynic—he was realistic. Nor did motives bother him, as long as they were honest. He was never anything but honest himself, and it would surprise him very much to know that those who filtered through his sometimes aloof existence respected that honesty and also found that it brought a boundless compassion. He liked life; he lived it vigorously and straightfor-wardly. When aroused, he was a formidable enemy. When dealt with on a level of his own integrity, he was capable of great chivalry, kindness, and generosity.

Her head bobbed up in the water near his, and he smiled with a lazy charisma. With that lustrous mane of shoulder-length chestnut hair wet and slicked back from her face, one thing was obvious: she had no interest in his finances. Her ears were stud-ded with small but flawless emeralds, and as she rose in the waist-high water, he saw that a slender link gold chain held a matching emerald oval in the deep shadowed cleavage of her breasts.

15

Why she was seeking him, he couldn't imagine. But it would have taken a far more monastic man than he to question such good fortune.

Their eyes met, and for a moment he again sensed that hint of tragedy. But her stare was direct. She wasn't playing cat and mouse.

"Hello," he said, his appreciation unabashed as he watched her at this closer angle. She was perfection. Her skin was lightly golden, as smooth as silk, from the enticing angles of her collarbone to the line of slightly visible ribs to the curve of her hips and tight, concave structure of her waist, navel, and upper abdomen. Someone, he thought idly, some great artist, should paint her image in oil one day, or preserve it forever in the marble she resembled.

"Hello," she returned, and the voice fit the woman. It was low, husky, and melodious, carrying just a hint of well-bred southern culture. Her single word was not aggressive, nor was it coy. That direct stare of hers had not once wavered, and yet he could sense a certain nervousness; he could see it now in the fine pulsation of a light blue vein in the swanlike structure of her neck.

Without his really realizing it, or exactly knowing why, Drake's smile became very gentle, his emotions turned to protection. "My name is Drake O'Hara," he told her, offering her a hand while longing to bring it around her shoulders and cradle her to him with a combination of overwhelming lust and tender care. Strange, that she could affect him so intensely.

She took his hand in her graceful, slender one. "I'm Ronnie."

She didn't offer a last name, and he didn't demand one. His grin broadened. "I think I say I'd like to buy you a drink now."

"I'd like that," she said. A bewitching impishness suddenly replaced that tragic look in her beautiful eyes. "Then I can say I'd like to buy you one."

"I'd like that," he told her huskily, shaken by the violence of the savage desire that ripped through him. He'd barely touched the woman. "I'll hop out and buy my round poolside," he added.

Ronnie couldn't quite manage to look into his face, but she

wanted her position clear from the beginning. They could share drinks; he could purchase a round, she could purchase a round. No debts, no commitment. "That's fine," she said softly. "I'll also buy mine poolside."

"Will you?"

His well-modulated voice had fallen a notch, and a chilling quiver of apprehension rippled through Ronnie, seeming to come from the coolness of the water. His two-word question had been a curious musing. He wanted to get to know her.

She couldn't get to know him; it was bad enough that she was coveting this experience so far . . . losing herself in the sight of him, in the sound of his voice. . . .

"I think I'd like you to buy me a drink before dinner." He raised a hand in amused proclamation of honor as she started to speak. "Just dinner," he said sincerely. "Will you?"

Dinner. Just dinner. "Yes," she said, her voice still soft but firm, with no guile. Her blue eyes raised from the water to meet his, yet they seemed an extension of the water they had left. They were like dazzling prisms, as myriad and brilliant as a star-studded night. It was hard to tell if they were as icy as a blizzard, or as warm and torrid as the blazing sun that crested high over the Atlantic.

Drake's eyes flicked only briefly. He had known from the moment he saw her that she was a cool woman of determined purpose. Still, the cloak she wore was an enigma, as mysterious as her stately beauty.

"What shall I bring you to drink?" he asked, his voice carrying that husky timbre he couldn't quite control.

It wasn't the type of question to cause confusion in such an independent lady, but it did. She frowned. "Oh, ah, I don't know. . . ."

"Piña coladas," he decided quickly, again surprised by the surge of protection that assailed him.

She visibly relaxed, making him realize just how overwrought she had been.

"A piña colada sounds lovely," she told him.

Drake wasn't fond of the rum and coconut drink himself, but to keep her company, he ordered two. It was, after all, a cruise.

The four-hundred-passenger cruise ship left Charleston Harbor Friday afternoon and would return to its berth early the following Monday morning. Three days of relaxation, with the majority of passengers being businessmen or professionals with little time to spare from hectic schedules. Drake had taken the time himself simply to unwind. He had imagined nothing more than a few hours of sun, fine food when the mood took him, and three peaceful nights rest upon the lull of the Atlantic. He hadn't come for companionship, but rather to avoid it.

And now this. But he was already thoroughly enchanted; he could have refused her no more than he could have asked the sun not to shine. They had spoken so little, but he was dimly aware that her soft, husky, southern-cultured voice would later seep into his dreams.

"A piña colada," he said, sitting poolside, his long, tanned legs dangling in the water. She smiled lightly at his return and hopped lithely from the water to join him. Her arm brushed his as she sat alongside him, their naked thighs touching. The contact was jolting, almost shattering, as if a jagged bolt of lightning had struck from a clear sky to sear through them both.

Ronnie inhaled a sharp breath, meeting Drake's dark gaze, perpetuating no pretense at the intensity of the purely physical pleasure she was experiencing. That which had been hidden away so long it had almost been forgotten, rose to the surface with a crippling poignancy. Just to be beside this man was excitement enough to send waves of heat washing through her—a heat that felt so damn good. She was, after all, a mature woman, so long denied. And even though the reason for her denial was a part of her heart, she couldn't fight this intrinsic beauty that had been granted her.

"Thank you," she said, taking the drink he offered her, once more aware of the beauty of the power of masculine hands. "To the cruise," she offered, tipping her glass to his.

"To the cruise," he repeated solemnly, his black eyes smoldering into pits of raven coal. A saint would be shaking on a pedestal with her so near. "And to you, Ronnie."

"Thank you," she murmured again, and he thought he perceived a soft blush. "Drake . . ." she said, in afterthought, seeming to twirl his name on her tongue as if she savored it. Averting her eyes for a moment, she took a sip of her drink. "Where are you from, Drake?" she queried.

He could have sworn she was somewhat anxious, which was peculiar, because conversation didn't really seem to interest her.

"The Midwest," he replied, sure that his answer pleased her. "Chicago. How about you?"

She smiled again, and this time the curl of her lips lit a true warmth into her eyes. "That's obvious, isn't it?" Her chuckle was as low and melodious as her voice.

"Yes, it is," he answered, his grin deepening to disclose a cleft in his chin she'd yet to discover. "But from where in the South?"

"Oh, ah—Georgia."

She was lying, but why? At this point he had no desire to challenge her. Sitting together, talking, was taking away the initial edge. She had tensed when she lied—a dead giveaway. But other than that, she had begun to truly relax in his presence, as if she had made a decision to trust him completely. Despite her cool sophistication, that trust drew out all his male instincts. Somewhere on a level beneath conscious thought, it was registering with him that she was all he had ever wanted in a woman. Assured yet reserved, aloof yet incredibly warm. He had the feeling that he had touched upon the tip of an iceberg—and that a wealth awaited him beneath the surface. That wealth would be a host of wonders—intelligence, loyalty, and wit to match her rare beauty and poise.

When she spoke, the mystical blue of her eyes was enchantment; when she laughed, it became a shimmering pool of the deepest enticement.

And yet she held that reserve, so he agreeably tread slowly. She shied from personal conversation; they discussed the world and society at large. Time, space, land. He wanted her more than he had ever wanted a woman, but he had never wanted more to woo a woman, to cajole and to please, to care for and to protect.

That evening it was dinner. Just dinner. When he left her at the door to her cabin, he barely brushed her lips.

His rewards were great—breakfast, lunch, and dinner, and delightful times in between, the next day. She hesitated each time she gave him a yes, as if she struggled inwardly. But he asked nothing of her. He was willing to wait for her, for whatever time she needed. He was planning on a long-range assault, and the stakes he slowly realized he was seeking were infinitely high.

Another night passed with his softly brushing her lips at her cabin door; a night that ended a day in which they had both veered from personal queries.

Talk and questions that delved could come later. They simply savored one another's company.

On Sunday afternoon they sat together by the pool again, uniquely comfortable in a companionable silence.

Ronnie's eyes were only half open as she regarded the water, dazzling as it rippled beneath the sun. She was being foolish, and she knew it. But she hadn't been able to refuse Drake, because she didn't want to. She closed her eyes tightly for a minute, against pain, against remorse, against guilt. It might be wrong to want to feel, to cherish this being alive and young and vibrant near this extraordinary man, but in the end, what difference did it make? She would never see him again; who could she hurt but herself?

And how much worse could she possibly hurt?

For years now she had learned to tolerate pain, withdrawing from it into an inner shell. She had learned to be strong; she had learned to turn her cheek. She had done it, because underneath it all she knew she was desperately needed . . . and despite all, still loved. And though her love had changed as the love given to her had, it was still there, along with the memories she could not betray.

This wasn't betrayal, her heart suddenly raged with a surge of rebellion that brought tears to her eyes. She deserved this little happiness she had found. Everyone needed something . . . or else they cracked. And she couldn't crack. No matter what, she couldn't crack. . . .

She was the wall that was leaned upon.

Except now, with Drake. It still made her slightly nervous to have his undivided masculine attention after having been denied such attention for so long. He held her arm, he took her hand, he guided. It was wonderful. It would be so easy to become accustomed to having his strength . . . to his taking any weight from her own shoulders. . . .

"What's wrong?" he suddenly asked, his perceptive dark gaze upon her with instant concern.

She blinked, marveling at how quickly he could read her slightest change of mood. She couldn't allow him to read her so well.

"The sun," she told him with a quick smile. "I left my glasses below."

He insisted they go and get them. She laughed and said she would go herself, but he was determined to accompany her, and he was a very difficult man to dissuade. Impossible, actually, to dissuade.

He followed her into her cabin, and she made a hasty show of searching for her sunglasses.

But suddenly she froze as she delved through a dresser. She could feel his eyes; she could feel his heat. He made no movement, he didn't touch her, but the very air of the cabin seemed charged with an electrical current that was naturally sensual, irrefutably real.

God, how she wanted him, needed him.

It was wrong. . . . It was a dream, yet she so desperately needed that dream.

She straightened, dropping all pretense. Their eyes met. And then, with no further thought, she shortened the space between them and flew into his arms.

They engulfed her, with love, with need, with security, with tenderness.

"Oh, Ronnie," he groaned hoarsely from his chest, "what do you want?"

"I want you to make love to me," she told him honestly, tilting her chin up at him with pride.

She was blatantly honest, beautifully honest, and as her gaze remained amazingly steady there was a tremulous hint of yearning in her tone. A sweet, sweet poignancy.

"Lady," he murmured, his whisper brushing over the top of her hair, "you have got me."

With standing impudence and warmth, her arms clung tighter, relishing in the feel of taut bronze muscles. They constricted and rippled at her touch, drawing a barely perceptible groan from him. Abashed at her brazen impetuousness, Ronnie slipped away for a moment, shaking her wet head in an effort to cover the crimson coloring that was sneaking up her cheeks. What must he think? That she was starved?

She was.

But though her honesty didn't bother her—she could never have played the scene with hypocritical coyness—the urgency that was building within her did. They had the rest of the day, the night. That was it—the dream would be over. It shouldn't matter what he thought of her, but it did.

"Ronnie."

His voice rang with a gentle command, and as she turned back to him, she saw that there was a tenderness in his coal-dark eyes. "You're wonderful," he told her gravely, his look emphasizing his sincerity. "Like a beautiful breath of fresh air. Please don't be ashamed. Not with me. I love it that you want me . . . that you come to me."

He extended his arms to her, and she rushed back to them, choking a sob as she buried her head into the crisp black hair of his chest, finding that sense of comfort in his powerful hold that she craved emotionally as her body craved his physically.

No, she would deny herself nothing today. She would take until she was satiated; she would give for all that she was worth. And then keep giving.

She tilted her head back with all this in the iridescence of her eyes. She brought her fingers to lock into the rich thickness of his black hair, touching it with devouring reverence. His eyes began to smolder once more as they bored into hers, still carrying that infinite tenderness. His lips touched upon hers softly, the touch of his mustache tickling delightfully. These things she savored sweetly for a cherishable moment, her own mouth pliant, her lips moistly parted. Then a brushfire began, a longing, a yearning, a needing, of such intensity that it stole her breath away. It took her from the confines of the cabin to a haven where sight, sound, and reality were all lost in abandon to one overwhelming sensation—him.

Drake too had obliterated all conscious thought that didn't have to do with the splendor in his arms. He had meant to be nothing but completely gentle, but the thirst of her response to his first soft touch inflamed his blood to boiling in heedless seconds. Her body molded to his as he kissed her, his tongue probing, plundering, and then ravishing. Never had he come across a woman of a more beautiful, natural sensuality. The satin of her skin was alive and warm, vibrant against him. Her breasts were pressed to his chest firmly, only the scanty bikini top separating the flesh that demanded to touch flesh. He fumbled for the tie as they locked together in that first devastating kiss. Slipping the offensive material away, he allowed it to fall haphazardly to the floor. A groan rumbled from deep within his throat as he felt her hardened nipples now press into his chest with exotic demand. His hands had to experience the pleasure. Fingers that had developed an extra sensitivity crept between the melded bodies to fondle and caress, circling, grazing, finding a firm fullness that swelled beneath his mastery.

He broke the kiss because he had to see her. He had to stare into the beautiful blue eyes that were dilated with passion, had to watch the rapid rise and fall of those perfect proud breasts, had to view with insatiable hunger the exoticism of still hardening, rose-tipped nipples beneath the play of his callused, foraging thumbs.

23

Funny that he had ever thought of her as marble. Marble was cool, cold to the touch. There was nothing cold about her. She was alive with titillating warmth, vibrant, vital, beautiful, breathing flesh and blood. . . .

"Exquisite," he gasped aloud, bringing forth from her a radiating sigh of sweet gratitude that was the most potent intoxication he could imagine. He lifted her into his arms, aware that his desire was raging out of control, but also aware that she needed that savage demand from him. And there was nothing that could ignite a man more than the sure knowledge that *he was* wanted as badly as he wanted. . . .

Although his body decried him, he had to pause as he slipped the bikini briefs from her undulating hips. Again, he had to see her. Against the starched white of the sheets, she was a golden goddess. Her waist, as he had known, was minuscule, her hips flared in a perfect curve, her breasts magnificent mounds of divinity. Her legs were uncanny, long, slender, majestically shapely. . . . His assessment was a slow, self-induced torture, but he couldn't tear his eyes away, not even with the anticipation of touching her again, of taking her as his own completely.

"Drake!" She called his name imploringly, arms outstretched, to break his hypnotic state. And she watched him with awe as he cast aside his own swim trunks to lower himself beside her.

She touched him without hesitancy, free of inhibition, weaving a spell upon him that would never be broken. He had never known a woman to offer so much, to elicit, to respond with such sweetly delicious abandon and unwavering passion. Their hands simultaneously explored what their eyes had discovered, and warmth was soon the blue-gold fire of a blazing inferno.

The forces that catapulted them into the spiraling whirlpool of heedless desire were brought to a primeval level. Man and woman, locked together in the oldest, most beautiful gift of the gods. And as in those times of old, it was man who had to conquer. Conquer with giving and taking the ultimate surrender.

Drake couldn't have recognized the feeling at the time, but his protective attitude had been joined by possessiveness. She had become his, and as if she could be in truth a prize sent from heaven for him alone, he sought to know her completely before establishing the claim that was bursting within him. His kisses, soft and explorative, greedy and demanding, rained down upon her. They circled her breasts, tasting the sweet nectar of chlorine mingled with that of her sweet self; they grazed over her hips, savoring the undulation, and over tender thighs that quivered in delight.

Ronnie thought she would soon go mad from the ecstasy he had created. He was so beautifully, magnificently male. So strong, so powerful, so overwhelming. She had forgotten these wonderful sensations that now engulfed her like the waves of the ocean. Her fingers dug into the breadth of his back, marveling at the shudders that convulsed his shoulders, heedlessly basking in their masterful command. She allowed herself the irresistible wonder of falling into the awesome spell of his compelling domination, almost fainting with sheer glory when he finally took her to himself as one.

But she was relentlessly taken from the moment of near oblivion, caught in a rhythm of stroking satin that demanded reciprocation. Cries tore from her throat as her body responded of its own volition, arching to his, writhing madly. His hands held her hips, guiding them to his will—held her still when they reached a simultaneous, ardent shattering, and she again seemed to lose consciousness for a few seconds, unable to assimilate completely the quivering wonder and beauty of their coming together in pure, delicious ecstasy.

Drake couldn't leave her, couldn't break the physical tie that bound them. Knowing that his weight crushed her, he still covered her body, his hands raking her hair as he whispered feverishly of how he adored her. His thumbs traced the exquisite sculpture of her face until he found the moistness of tears, and then, only then, did he finally pull away to look at her with tender curiosity, his heart wrenched apart.

"My God, Ronnie," he murmured heatedly, "have I hurt you?"

"Oh, no!" she cried vehemently, encircling him with slender arms and drawing their bodies back together. "You are the most wonderful thing I have ever known. Please, keep holding me. . . ." She smiled through that mist of tears, and he obligingly held her, comforting her now with security, smoothing back her tousled hair, soothing her with fingers that lightly stroked the contours of her back.

"I think I'm in love," he mused gently, aloud, amazed at the emotions she could create in his bewildered heart and mind.

She stiffened in his arms for a moment and relaxed. "Is that possible?" she asked softly. "If it is, then I too am in a kind of love." Abruptly she pulled from him, only to set herself above him on his chest, her huge blue eyes looking beseechingly into his. "May I have the night, Drake? Will you be mine until the sun rises in the morning?" Her tone was wistful and almost whimsical.

"I think I may be yours for eternity," he told her, bewitched by her loveliness and the honest poignancy of her sad plea.

Ronnie buried her face into the black mat of his chest, inhaling his scent deeply to ingrain it forever in her memory. The hair tickled her skin, and she rubbed her cheek against it. The moment was a dream, pure illusion, but she couldn't stop herself from cherishing that dream, from perpetuating it.

"Will you be strong and tender and gentle forever?" she inquired impishly, leaning to kiss his lips and delightedly feel the tingle of his mustache.

"I can't promise gentle forever," he told her gravely in return. "There is something about you that makes me feel very fierce. But whatever strength and tenderness I have are yours."

Ronnie smiled again and sighed contentedly, nestling back into his chest. Tomorrow would bring despair, but she would welcome that despair to have this day . . . and this night to sleep beside this man. It was much more than she had bargained for, much more than she could have possibly imagined. And she would let nothing break this spell of enchantment. Not the torture of ifs, not the tremor of conscience.

They spent hours in her cabin, sometimes quietly lying beside one another, sometimes making love. They were slow and teasing and gentle, they were insatiably wild. And inevitably they talked, and in her dream world Ronnie answered questions without really answering. He knew a lot about her, but he really knew nothing. And it wasn't important. Facts could come later. He knew the things a lover should know—her smile, her touch, her mind, her heart.

They left the cabin as evening fell, hunger driving them to an intimate dinner with neither aware of other passengers around them. Dressed impeccably, they were the envy of all eyes that alighted upon them, eyes that believed in the illusion. They were an incredibly handsome couple, he unerringly masculine, she the epitome of feminine beauty and sophistication.

They were regal, their devotion charming. To anyone, they appeared as honeymooners, lost in the star-swept skies of their love, and in the Atlantic night. In mutual silence they toured the deck of the ship, basking in the lulling romance of the ocean breezes that leant enchantment to the illusion, and then returned to Ronnie's cabin, to delight in the pleasure of removing impeccable clothing.

And to make love into the night.

Drake slept well, satiated as he had never been in his life. His first statement had been playful—he had never really been in love. But now he was convinced—with a definite shade of bemusement—that he was. And the feeling was wonderful. As he held her to him, he wondered for the first time in his life how it would be to sleep and to awaken with this exquisite creature at his side every day of his life. He had thought he could never endure such monotony—but with Ronnie there would never be monotony. Only increasing wonder and discovery; increasing commitment and devotion.

He had no doubts that they had only begun something beautiful. She was still a marble beauty, reserved and—statuesque— when she walked and talked and moved. But in his arms she was radiant, a warm and sensuous woman. Only for him; the type he hadn't believed existed—a creature utterly lovely, utterly bright, and utterly worthy of trust. Cynicism that had bordered on the edge of any previous relationships had nothing to do with this one.

He actually wanted to marry her. Now. Not even having known her for more than the past three days. Not even having learned her last name. He didn't want to contemplate the idea of her ever being touched again by another man.

Drake O'Hara—playboy, cynic, hardened rogue of midwestern society—had fallen in love. It had come like a thunderbolt, but it was as sure as the moon in the night sky. And he did not deny the emotion, instead he reveled in it . . . mulling it over and over in his mind with awe.

That the beauty who had captured his heart with a single winning smile could be indulging in only a brief affair never occurred to him. She was too giving, too open, too willing. Too honestly passionate and caring.

And too often she had whispered and cried in the throes of passion that she too loved him. And so he slept well.

Ronnie didn't sleep through the night.

Not because she reflected on the misery of daybreak, but because she didn't want to lose one precious moment of having him beside her, of looking at him, of feeling the vibrancy of his rugged flesh touching hers. She memorized the planes of his face, with her eyes, with her fingers. She would never forget the depth of his dark-brown eyes; the twitch of his mustache when he half-smiled, and its grazing over her skin, sending shivers racing through her.

She had been starved; she was now sated. Still she would take more, even when that taking was lying awake through the night to absorb him—his scent, his feel, his breathing, his face in sleep. A tender smile lit her lips. Sound asleep, he was still imposing. The lines that were etched faintly around his eyes were relaxed, but he still looked formidable, as if his dark eyes could fly open at any minute and challenge with ferocity, as if his muscled length could spring instantly to action. She knew the strength of those muscles, but to her they were nothing but powerfully gentle.

Inevitably, morning came. Still she watched him, and when he did open his eyes, she made no effort to hide her surveillance.

She wanted to have him love her one last time.

The message was in her eyes, and he did love her, taking her into his arms naturally without words. The words came later as he caressed her; they were endearments. Then they were groaned commands; groans from the exotic pleasure that she gave him, and then fervent whispers that were returned with breathless moans.

Waking up was all that he had dreamed it would be. And holding her close after their tumultuous sharing was nothing but sheer, ultimate wonder, and the intimacy of helping her shower and dress, nothing but the contentment of a lifetime.

They would breakfast, and then the ship would dock.

Over coffee and toast, it was time for the facts. But before he could begin to ask she gave him her steady gaze and placed her slender hand over his. "Thank you, Drake. Thank you for this piece of heaven," she told him in her soft, melodious voice.

"Thank you?" He chuckled low in inquiry. "Babe, thank you for being! But our piece of heaven is just beginning."

She frowned and lowered her murky lashes, but not before he sensed the tragedy again in the depths of her crystal-blue eyes. When she looked up again, all warmth was gone from them. He was staring into ice.

"This was just a cruise, Drake. It's over," she told him firmly.

"Over?" His demand was harsh and guttural. He could feel his infamous temper rising in an uncontrollable flash. What was her game? His hand came over hers to grasp it ruthlessly. "What are you talking about?"

Ronnie didn't flinch, nor did she allow her gaze to waver, although she felt as if her insides were melting beneath the burning fury of coal that bored into her. She had never thought she could be afraid of him, of anyone for that matter, and yet she was frightened. It occurred to her belatedly that she had trifled with a man one didn't trifle with. But she couldn't have wanted any other, she couldn't have had her night of magic. She couldn't have fallen in love.

And she was in love, but she knew the tangles and variants of love. She was in love, and in love with being in love. It was precious, to be locked away in her mind and heart to sustain her.

But love was also something else; something else that was mutable, but irrevocable nonetheless. It was—oddly enough—loyalty and devotion even when the stars had long ceased to shine. It was enduring. It was emotional stamina.

"It's over," she repeated numbly.

"No." Drake denied her roughly. "You gave yourself to me completely last night. And I want you. I have no intention of letting you go."

Ronnie's chuckle was brittle, dry, and very bitter. "I'm sorry. I can't be your permanent mistress."

His grip upon her intensified until she was sure her bones would crack. In a moment the dark flames of his eyes would combust into hot red flames, and she would be staring directly at the devil.

"Mistress, woman! Be damned. I want to marry you!"

Her eyes fell. She could no longer face him. When she spoke, it was tonelessly, as if she were very far away.

"I can't marry you, Drake."

For a moment he eased, sensing pain beneath the jagged-glass hardness of her eyes and voice. There was something in her past that had created the glacial reserve that she could hide behind. But he didn't care what it was. He wanted to protect her, to nurture her, to guide her into a world of comfort and happiness.

"I'm rushing you," he said smoothly, and when she glanced at him again, she felt her heart catch in her throat. He was so handsome and virile before her in his perfectly tailored tan suit, the sleek darkness of his hair and eyes and the healthy glow of his tanned ruddy skin emphasized by its cool lightness. The arch of his brows was high as his lips twitched the corners of his mustache in a half-smile. The cooling arrogance of his temper was still discernible, but it was mellowed now to a sure command.

"Ronnie," he continued, rubbing a finger over the veins of her hand, "there are no can'ts, except that I can't let you go. You have to trust me, as you did when we met. I know you're fighting something, but I'll help you. I don't care about your past. I don't care about your present. I'll work mine into it. I don't believe that you don't care about me—as much as I care about you, no matter how ludicrous it is after only three days. I'll go as slow as you like. But you have to keep seeing me. I'll never convince you of my sincerity otherwise."

A torrent of sobs welled in her rib cage, threatening to spill forth. She had to build the wall, retreat, and then get away surely and quickly. The angle of his jawline was square and determined; nothing but the cold truth would keep him away, and she would have to risk his contempt whether it devastated her or not.

She withdrew her hand from his and picked up her coffee cup with cool dismissal. "Drake, I can't—repeat, can't—continue to see you. It's out of the question."

"Really?" An imperious brow arched even higher, and his lips tightened into a caustic line. "And why not? What happened to I love you and forever?"

I do love you, Ronnie whispered to herself sadly, *but you'd never understand, and even if you did, I could never explain. . . .*

She took a sip of coffee and set the cup down briskly. "Oh, come, Drake," she said, "surely a man such as yourself has had his share of flings! Love is just a word. So is forever."

"We didn't spend a day and night exchanging words," he told her sardonically, drawing the hint of a hoped-for blush. No one could make love as she had without feeling!

But his angel of the night had turned back to marble by day. "We played the game to make something pretty of a physical attraction," she said cuttingly. With a wry and glacial smile she added, "To spend a night making love sounds much nicer than spending a night having sex!"

She hadn't anticipated what happened next. He set his iron-

31

clad fingers around her wrist and drew her to her feet in an undeniable gesture that was barely civilized despite the crowd in the dining room. He didn't stop for a second as he led, or rather dragged, her down the corridor and back to her cabin, ignoring her comments, whether they were demanding, angry, or scornful.

He stopped inside the cabin, after he had slammed the door and pinned her to it, claiming her lips, plundering her mouth savagely. His hands moved over territory he knew by heart, aggressively taunting, cradling breasts that were his, searching beneath material to find the answer he expected—flesh that heated to his touch, nipples that grew taut on contact.

Ronnie furiously pummeled against him and twisted her head to avoid his kiss. But his lips were clamped on hers. Her comparatively feeble struggles had no effect on his steellike determination to have his way. Her protests were muffled as his teeth grazed hers, pitted against them, and his tongue found the access to probe her mouth with heady command. Ronnie's attempt at words died, her mouth gave sweetly to his. She would never be able to deny him. A moment later she was arched against his chest, moaning as his fingers worked their spell upon her, twisting at the peak of her breast to send chills of pleasure racing down her spine as he held her in that relentless embrace.

Then he pulled away from her, using his hands and arms as inescapable bars around her. Eyes that were as dark as night seared into hers with ruthless demand.

"Now tell me again that this all means nothing to you," he grated harshly, his breathing as strained as hers.

She was shaking, panting, unnerved. God help her, she couldn't cry. But a lie would not suffice.

"All right!" she flashed in answer to his challenge. "It means something. It means something very wonderful. But it can't be!"

"Why not?" He would not soften now. He wanted answers. The ship was docked in Charleston Harbor. Time was running out. "Ronnie, I want to marry you."

A sob did tear from her throat. "I can't marry you!" she cried, the ice finally melting from her eyes as they stared tremulously into his. "I can't marry anyone. I'm already married."

But she wasn't! her heart cried out.

She was, for all intents and purposes. Discovering the false validity of a piece of paper didn't change anything. And yet she knew in the back of her mind, no matter how irrevocable the future, that the discovery had allowed her this wonderful day. She had used it to rationalize her actions. . . .

Legally, she was free.

But her freedom was empty; the ties that bound her had never had anything to do with legalities.

And none of it could ever be explained to Drake, who stared at her now with deep, piercing fury. . . .

"I am married," she repeated aloud, wrenched from the pain of longing by the staunch reminder to herself of what must be.

Drake emitted a single, explosive oath. If he had been burned to cinders by the roaring heat of lava, he couldn't have been more shocked or wounded. He had been duped in the worst way possible; he had given everything to someone else's *restless* wife. Trust, he thought cynically, as his arms dropped to his sides. What a fool. He had thought he had found the one woman he could love, cherish, and trust eternally.

He stepped away from her, still looking into her eyes, now seeing nothing but traitorous blue; magnificent, treacherous, radiant blue.

He had been used by a conniving witch he had deemed the soul of honesty.

The look alone that he gave her could have shattered a shell of lighter stuff. But even as she felt herself agonizingly ripped asunder inside, as if her heart had been torn from her body, Ronnie stood still.

Composed as marble.

If he touched her again, she would break. But he didn't touch her. She had the feeling that he controlled his temper because he feared what he might do if he let it loose. His hands were balled

33

into fists at his sides, his broad shoulders appeared imposingly massive. But it was his dark face that set her blood racing. His glowering eyes were daggers; his mouth a white line of condemnation. His teeth were clenched together; she could see the twisted angle of his jaw as he ground them against each other.

She wanted to throw herself into his arms and explain. It was unbearable that he hate her so. But for all the rogue she had assessed him to be, she learned swiftly now that he was a man of certain morals. Affairs were fine. Extramarital affairs were unthinkable.

If she could explain, if there was any way—which there wasn't —it would be senseless to fly to him anyway. He would cast her aside as tarnished goods. Her situation was too incredulous to believe or to understand.

Her hands were behind her on the door. She braced them now, for support. "I think you should leave now, Drake."

"As you wish," he replied glacially. "Mrs. uh . . . ?"

"It doesn't matter," Ronnie said blandly, praying he would leave.

"It does matter, Ronnie," he told her gravely. But he didn't press the point. Instead he reached for her arm and pulled her from the door, dropping her arm again quickly after he had moved her out of his way. His touch had been as red-hot as a branding iron.

He stopped for only a second to gaze back at her. "Oh—thank you for a most interesting cruise."

Then he was gone. His piercing gaze, his towering disdain, were all that remained imprinted on her mind. Her knees buckled beneath her and she slid to the floor, gripping her stomach as if he had dealt her a blow with a two-by-four.

But still she didn't cry. She sat rocking, biting her lip. They were calling the passengers ashore. She pulled herself back to her feet by grasping the bedpost. After walking into the cabin's small bathroom, she splashed her face with cool water and made a few makeup repairs, her hands moving mechanically. She curled her hair into a tight bun at the back of her neck and donned sunglasses and a chic, wide-brimmed beige felt hat that matched her smart heels and small sling handbag.

Gathering her things, she left the cabin. But not without looking back at the still-rumpled bed.

She had never intended to; it had been foolish. But she had fallen in love. The precious memories were the ones she would learn to recall, not those of his dark ferocity at her deception. She would learn to remember his eyes as they blazed the tender fire of passion, not the charred embers of scorn.

And in the loneliness of her austere existence, she would sort out the misery of the different types of love. Her tears would come later. Upon the remote windswept island that was her home, she would find ample time for solace. And she would be plunged back into grueling reality.

The woman the world knew as Mrs. Pieter von Hurst walked away from her breakaway cruise, her heels clicking briskly upon the deck.

The immaculate sophisticated lady.

Beautiful, poised, reserved, genteel—yes, the perfect, seldom-seen wife of the world's most brilliant contemporary sculptor.

And one of the most unhappy women alive.

CHAPTER TWO

It was amazing that the sea could change so quickly. It had been calm, glassy, and cobalt-blue for the cruise, serene beneath powdery skies.

Now it matched Ronnie's mind. Foam-flecked waves were pulsating in wild whipped peaks, rising with the whistling of the wind. The sky was losing its early-morning glow, growing gray with a vengeance.

"Storm's blowin' in," Dave Quimby announced unnecessarily, pulling his yellow slicker cap lower over his forehead. He scratched his grizzled beard and gave Ronnie a gap-toothed smile. "Maybe ye'd best head on in to the cabin, Miss Veronica."

Ronnie shook her head and smiled back with affection. Dave, her husband's fulltime captain—a necessity when one lived on one's own island miles off the the shore of Charleston—was her one true friend in her home of five years. He was a man unintimidated by Pieter von Hurst; if he feared and respected anything, it was only the sea. To his credit, Pieter respected and admired Dave.

And if Dave cared for any human being with a degree of his softer nature, it was Pieter's young wife. She might be the courteous Mrs. von Hurst to the rest of the world, but to Dave she was Miss Veronica, as she had been on that day long ago when Von Hurst had returned to the island to stay as a recluse forever.

Dave sensed more than most people. He had known from the beginning that there was something very wrong with his employer's marriage. Brides were supposed to be happy, radiant young

36

things. Miss Veronica had never been happy—not since the day she stepped ashore and looked over the barren island with a deep sigh of resignation. Only he had seen the dejection in her eyes. When Von Hurst had snapped something at her, she had turned to him with a gentle, tolerant smile.

Of course, Von Hurst was sick. Much sicker than most folks knew. If Dave's intuitions were right, Von Hurst was dying. *And God forgive me,* Dave thought, *the sooner the man dies the better.*

Better for the gentle mistress he loved.

Ronnie shook her head at Dave. "I don't want to go below!" she called above the roar of the Boston Whaler's engines and the wind. "I love the sea like this!"

He grinned knowingly. Maybe he loved her because she loved the sea as he did—and because she was like a storm at sea. Her true nature always hidden, unless she was out with him, Miss Veronica had depths as fathomless as the Atlantic, as tumultuous as any gale that blew. Only with him was she like a nymph of Neptune, her feet scampering over planks with excitement when they sailed, her head lifted to the wind. She was always willing to fight the roughest weather.

The sea was her escape.

Too soon they reached the jagged shore of Von Hurst's island. "Go on up to the house, Miss Veronica," Dave yelled over the encroaching wind. "You look too pretty to get a drenching! I'll get your things up right away."

"Thanks, Dave," Ronnie said, slipping her bare feet back into her heels. The pathway to the gray brick manor loomed before her, and she had no choice but to follow it. Resecuring strands of hair as she walked, she made her way along the gravel, her footsteps sure and determined. At the double oak doors she rang the bell; the house was always locked, although their nearest neighbor was islands away. Curiosity seekers sometimes motored too near.

"Good morning, Henri," Ronnie greeted the elderly butler and companion to her husband. "Where is Mr. von Hurst?"

Removing her hat and gloves, Ronnie queried him with the formal propriety that was expected of her. "Is he in his studio?"

"No, Mrs. von Hurst," Henri replied, equally formal. "Mr. von Hurst had a poor night. He is in his sitting room. He did, however, request that you come to him immediately upon your return home."

"Thank you," Ronnie said, walking sedately down the hallway to the spiral staircase. She didn't want to see Pieter—and she hadn't expected that he would want to see her right away. She had wanted to go straight to her own room and lie down and sleep and dream and preserve her memories. . . .

But this was better. Pieter was right. They had to face each other; they had to break the ice that must surely exist between them now.

She paused before the door to his sitting room and forced her hand to knock upon the varnished wood. She always knocked. There were times when Pieter wouldn't allow her near him; when he couldn't bear the sight of her.

"Come in."

Pushing open the door, Ronnie quietly entered her husband's darkened sitting room and stood still, waiting for him to turn and speak to her as he stood at his own vigil at the huge bay window. Obviously he had been awaiting her return; he had watched her walk up the gravel path.

He was silent for several minutes, his hands clasped behind his back, his tall form pathetically emaciated. But at least he wasn't in the chair today, Ronnie thought, her heart constricting with the pity she was careful never to show. He was standing straight, his parchment skin tight across a countenance that had never been handsome but still carried a nobility, despite the ravages of illness.

A shudder rippled violently through her as she watched his back and remembered their last encounter. He had been wild on that day, adamant, telling her he no longer needed to seek a divorce because he had discovered, in his attempts to obtain one, that their marriage was illegal. The "notary" who had performed the ceremony hadn't been a notary at all. . . .

Pieter had been so hard, so cruel. But she knew his motives. In his way he did love her, and he feared he was reaching the end. After five years, he had decided to cause her no more pain.

But she knew he needed her more than ever now, and she could be just as adamant as he. "Forget it, Pieter," she had told him stubbornly. "Even if you're telling me the truth, it makes no difference. I've been your wife for five years."

He had bluntly assured her he was telling the truth. And he had insisted upon the cruise. A taste of freedom might be the answer.

Ronnie understood him. To placate him, she agreed. Yet she had never bargained on meeting Drake.

"Well?" Pieter queried her abruptly without turning. "You went?"

"Yes."

"And?" His form twisted a degree as he waited for her answer.

"It was a pleasant little vacation," she replied simply.

"Good," he replied brutally. "Perhaps you'll see some sense."

"No, Pieter," she replied, her voice barely above a whisper. "I will not leave you. Nor will I allow you to cast me out."

Her words rushed sweetly to his ears, but he closed his eyes in pain. "You'll do as I say, Ronnie," he replied harshly. She didn't reply, and he almost smiled as he imagined the stubborn tilt of her jaw. Maybe she was happy. . . . *Happy.* The thought was ludicrous. Not after the years he had inadvertently put her through. . . .

"That's all, Ronnie," he clipped rudely.

His bony shoulders seemed to hunch forward for a moment with weakness, and Ronnie had to prevent herself from rushing to him. Now, more than ever, he would want none of her compassion. She stood quietly, suddenly feeling very ill herself but, although dismissed, determined to keep a fearful eye on him for the next few minutes. When the pause between them became unendurable, she ventured a question.

"Will we be working today?" She braced herself, in case he became angry. She had to stay by him, but she had already pushed him today with her determination to do so. . . . And her guilt was weighing heavy on her mind. She knew the facade he wore. Beneath it, he was a good man.

She curled her fingers into her fists, not noticing that the nails dug deeply into her flesh. In her own mind she was still his wife. She had entered the marriage, whether valid or not, with open eyes. And still she had grasped for her little piece of the moon. . . . God forgive her, but she had had to have it. . . .

"No, we won't be working today. I do not feel that I could do the marble justice." He finally turned from the window and stared at her with somber eyes. She realized he was trying to smile. "Nor could I do justice to you today, my dear."

Ronnie felt the ever-threatening tears welling in her eyes. If only he had been cruel, flown into one of his tantrums! A small sob escaped her and she left the doorway to come to his side, but he stopped her with a hand in the air, his eyes closing.

"No, Ronnie, please," he murmured. "I—I want to be alone. Tomorrow we will go back to work."

Ronnie halted stiffly in mid-stride, swallowed, and nodded. "Can I do anything for you?" she asked softly.

"No, I'm fine. Go to your room and rest. Tomorrow we will be receiving a house guest. You will have your hostess duties to attend to when we are not in the studio." For now, anyway, he was informing her that they would go on as usual.

Ronnie nodded again. "Who is coming?"

"The gallery owner who will be handling the marble pieces." Pieter gave her a crooked grin reminiscent of better times; times when he had been a young and sound man. "He's quite a tyrant, I hear, determined to light a fire under the great Pieter von Hurst. A fine connoisseur of the arts, and a ruthless business tycoon to boot. You'll have to be your most charming—and determined to spare me his lectures."

Ronnie smiled. "We'll keep him at bay."

Pieter suddenly sagged into the massive wing chair by the

window. Once more, Ronnie would have rushed to him, but he stopped her again with a hard stare and an uplifted hand. "Go now, Ronnie," he said gruffly.

Squaring her shoulders, she turned and walked softly to the door.

"Ronnie?"

"Yes?" She turned back to him quickly, surprised by the tenderness in his voice.

Absurdly Pieter von Hurst was momentarily tongue-tied. He looked over the exquisite beauty of the wife who could never be his, and he knew, as he always knew, despite his often atrocious behavior, that she had a beauty that went far beyond her regal physical attributes. Hers was of the mind, the heart, and the soul. He owed her so much! Rebellious and spirited herself, she quelled her own righteous anger when he bitterly raged into her, using her as a scapegoat when he sank into despair and lost control.

She had stuck by him through everything, maintaining the public image that was all he had left of a once-great pride, even when they had found out that the ceremony binding them together had been a sham, presided over by an unlicensed notary. In one of his moods created by fear, Pieter had practically ordered her from him. But Ronnie had understood, and remained solidly at his side. They had lived together as Mr. and Mrs. Pieter von Hurst for five years, she had told him. She was his wife. In the very near future they would reconcile the illegalities. . . .

"Ronnie," Pieter repeated, the thin, cracked line of his lips forming a bittersweet smile. "I know this is hard to believe, but I do love you."

"And I love you, Pieter," she answered softly.

"I know that, and I appreciate it. I . . . er . . . hope your cruise was nice." He had, compelled by ego, insisted she take the cruise before they "reconciled the legalities." "We won't speak about it again."

Ronnie nodded and moved swiftly for the door, unable to meet his ravaged eyes. She knew what his words had cost him, and the fact that he had spoken them was more than she could bear on top of everything else.

"Oh, Ronnie."

She paused with her hand on the door, not looking back.

"I . . . uh . . . missed you. Is it good to be home?" For Pieter, it was quite a speech.

"Wonderful." She strove for enthusiasm in her tone, but the word still came out as a whisper. Forcing herself to composure until she could sedately open and close the door, Ronnie then tore down the hall to her own room and locked herself in, a cascade of tears finally falling in torrents of silent misery as she was at last able to throw herself into the peaceful, private depths of her huge fur-covered four-poster bed.

A bed she had never shared with her "husband."

Ronnie had met Pieter von Hurst in Paris. She was just twenty-two, in love with spring, in love with Paris, and in love with Jamie Howell, one of Pieter's specially selected students. Few were so honored, few were lucky enough to study with the man, the artist, who was already considered a master though still in his early forties.

Von Hurst was rich and famous; he moved in the elite circles of society, from the Continent to the States. But Ronnie knew he had a fondness for her from the moment he met her. He had told her she was charming, eager, and brilliantly attuned to life, and had hosted the young couple to many a dance and dinner, reveling in their youth and enthusiasm.

And he was there when her talented fiancé fell prey to one of the oldest hazards of youth and the artistic community—heroin. Jamie was dead before Ronnie ever discovered the demon that had hounded him.

Ronnie was aware also that Pieter found her desirable, but he did not take advantage of her fresh innocence and beauty. He had made it very clear that he simply wanted to care for her. And she had let him. She was an American orphan, alone in Paris, grieved and bewildered, but already forming that shell of poised reserve that would hide her emotions from the world. She had been working as an interpreter for English-speaking tourists, but Pieter's artistic eye discovered a way to care for her and benefit them both. She would become his model, he reasoned, and the world also would benefit because her unearthly beauty would be forever captured in marble.

Although rumor ran rampant, she never did become his mistress. It was apparent that his love for her grew, as hers did for him. But she always knew her love for him was different. He was her friend, her mentor, a paternal figure. The difference in their ages was vast. But he wanted to marry her anyway. He had argued that he could make her love change.

And then three weeks before the wedding that was to be one of the grandest in Europe, Pieter found out about the disease that would rob him of his manhood—and eventually his life. Disbelieving and astounded, he railed against fate and cursed all who came near, never admitting the cause of his horrendous rages.

Except to Ronnie. He had told her, feebly offering her the release he couldn't bear, but she wouldn't go. And then it was he who turned to her for strength, she who salvaged the artist, Pieter von Hurst, she who gave him back to the world—at the cost of her own happiness and life.

But she did love him. When her own world had fallen to pieces, he had been there to pick her up. He had given her himself. She could give no less.

After a very quiet wedding—recently proved *too* quiet!—they quit Paris society and retired to the small island Pieter owned off the coast of South Carolina. Ronnie knew he could not bear for the public that idolized him to see him dissipate into a shrunken old man, long before his time.

She accepted interviews. She gave the papers the story of a perfect, complete marriage, of a one-to-one commitment that sent them scurrying into privacy to devote themselves to one another and to his art. And because of her, he did keep creating; he did find a reason to go on living.

At first there had been a natural fondness between them. The little that they had been able to share Pieter accepted—her touch, her lips, the glory of her beauty. But after the first six months of their self-imposed exile, his mind began to warp, the ravages of bitterness clouding all reason. To have Ronnie as his wife but *not* to have her, sent him reeling into a world of cruelty and anger. He lashed out at her constantly for no reason. Twice he had thrown things at her, drawing blood from her golden satinlike skin.

And still Ronnie tolerated him. She knew he would be contrite, knew she could never leave him. He needed her. And he did love her as he so often told her. She was a heaven-sent angel. He couldn't have made it without her then, but now he had acquired her strength and wisdom from their years together.

In his more lucid moments he had confessed that he also knew he had robbed her of her life, or at least of her youth. He told her that after his death, she would be well taken care of; she would be exorbitantly wealthy. But he was aware that money meant little to her, and that she was fiercely independent. Upon her insistence, the bulk of his estate had been left to world charities that benefitted children.

The recent passage of her twenty-ninth birthday had been more of a milestone for him than for her. He had finally been able to reach from his web of self-absorption to realize what he had done—sacrificed her for himself. She had uncomplainingly given him life, while he took hers. He had stifled all the joyous youth that had been rightfully hers.

And he had become determined to set her free, although it was proving a difficult task. She fought him, but he persisted in her taking the cruise, that she at least taste the pleasantries of life away from him and the depressing manor. She was impatient at his insistence, adamant against him, but he forced her to go. He repeated the same argument he had used for wanting the divorce. Her time for youth and love had been all too brief. He could live as a cripple for years to come. And if she refused to leave him, then she needed to have a season of happiness to recall when he inevitably took his turns for the worse. And though she knew that the bitterness ripped him apart at times, he fervently hoped that she would have a wonderful time.

Ronnie cried herself to sleep.

She woke to a crisp tapping on her door. "Just a minute!" she called out, aware that she was a sight. Springing into the bathroom, she washed her tear-stained face, resolving that she would have no more excursions into self-pity. Pieter must never know how wretched she was, nor how his insistence on the cruise had only made it all worse. No one knew the seriousness of his condition—except herself and his doctor. And she could weave illusion for him when others believed that he had a weak constitution, common among brilliant artists.

She had long ago schooled herself against tears. Only the cruise had brought them to the surface. They would have to be shelved again, with the new love that she had found.

Combing her hair back into its neat knot, she walked into her bedroom and called, "Come in."

Henri opened the door and stepped inside, a silver tray in his stiff arms. "Good evening, madam. Mr. von Hurst suggested I bring you a tray. He didn't think you'd feel up to dinner, nor did he desire to dine downstairs. I hope you find this satisfactory."

"Yes, fine, Henri," Ronnie said. "Thank you."

Henri nodded, his head as stiff as his arms. "Where would you like the tray, Mrs. von Hurst?"

For a whimsical moment Ronnie was tempted to tell him she'd like to see it dumped upon his proper head. In the five years of their living beneath the same roof he had yet to address her as anything except madam or Mrs. von Hurst. In this house, she mused, it was easy to forget she had been given a first name, much less a nickname. Pieter spent days enclosed when he didn't see her; when he did see her, often as not he didn't address her at all. The earlier encounter had been unique.

Ronnie did not tell Henri to dump the tray on his head. Instead she bit back the giddy smile that tinged her lips and replied properly, "Set it on the low table, please, Henri. I'll get to it in a minute."

"As you say, madam." Henri set the tray down as directed, clicked his heels with a little bow, and left her.

Ronnie could smell a delicious aroma drifting from the tray, and she was sure that Gretel, their surprisingly wraithlike cook, had intuitively prepared something to especially tempt her palate. Lifting the cover of the tray, she found a light and fluffy spinach soufflé. One of her favorite meals, as Gretel was well aware.

But Ronnie could do no more than pick at her food. Her head was spinning and, consequently, her stomach was churning. She should never have sought out Drake. She should have lied to Pieter.

The emotions and desires she had suppressed for years were now plaguing her with a vengeful agony. Touching her lips, she wondered if she imagined it, or if she could still really taste the sweet salt of Drake's kiss, if his scent still lingered on her own skin. . . .

She had known from the beginning that the cruise could only be a disaster. She had tried to tell Pieter, but he had become so agitated that she feared he would cause himself to have another attack, and so she had agreed, stricken that he should heap this new, inadvertent torment upon her. She had left, intending to come home cheerfully with a tan, assuring him she was complacent with her own world.

Then she had seen Drake. And in frank honesty she had simply wanted him. It had never occurred to her that the experience could so badly shatter her day-to-day existence.

Impatiently she set her fork down and gave up on the soufflé. She just couldn't eat. The memory of a previous shared meal was too close.

So as not to hurt Gretel's feelings, Ronnie guiltily flushed the remainder of the meal down the toilet. Then she unpinned her hair and climbed into the shower, making the water as hot as she could endure it, before scrubbing herself from head to toe and lathering her hair twice, soaking it in the expensive rinse Pieter ordered for her each month from Paris.

She desperately wanted to rid herself of the haunting masculine after-shave that seemed to cling to her body. The scent was driving her crazy; its intoxicating appeal wrenching her apart, creating longings that could not be fulfilled again.

The shower helped, and then she had things to do. After slipping into a set of Chinese lounging pajamas, Ronnie sat at her desk and planned a retinue of meals for the days to come, mulling over the proper wines for each with great care. She and Pieter entertained for only two reasons: Pieter's art, and his determination to create a living legend. Every guest was special; indeed, they entertained a number of dignitaries throughout the year.

If an arrogant tycoon had been invited to stay, Pieter wanted him impressed, no matter what his own feelings were. He was allowed to be moody or rude—he was the artist. Ronnie was supposed to create the atmosphere of genteel southern hospitality, to smooth all ruffled feathers. Pieter liked to be envied for his lovely wife. She was part of the elegance with which he surrounded himself.

Chewing on the nub of her pencil, Ronnie decided to have the Blue Room opened for this dubious guest's stay. The room was exceedingly masculine, its decoration basically stained wood paneling. The bed was a firm king-size, and the fireplace a very macho brick. Macho brick for a macho tycoon. That sounded good. And settled.

She picked up some of the correspondence that had accumulated but she couldn't concentrate on the letters. She dropped them again and picked up a book by one of her favorite authors and climbed beneath the cool silk sheets.

But she couldn't concentrate on the words. They kept blurring before her eyes, and the heroine was having a perfect love affair. If there was anything she didn't want to read about at that moment, it was a perfect love affair.

47

Ronnie snapped off her bedside lamp and curled into position to sleep. But try as she would, sleep would not come. Instead an image of dark eyes kept coming to her, and the memory of tender hands that demanded as they seduced.

Just last night it had all been real. And the reality was so strong now that she felt she could reach out and touch Drake. . . .

But she couldn't. All she could do was toss and writhe and close her eyes to dream—and burn with the sweet, simple memory of being held and cherished through the night.

It was very late when exhaustion finally overtook her and allowed her a few brief hours of respite.

Morning was much better. She had things with which to keep herself occupied. Pieter did not appear for breakfast, and she assumed correctly that he was saving his strength. As she had also expected, he sent her a crisp note by way of Henri, telling her that, after all, they would spend none of the day working. Dave would be motoring their guest to the island at five o'clock precisely—she should please see to it that she was dressed and prepared to greet him.

"Do you wish to reply, Mrs. von Hurst?" Henri asked politely.

"Yes," Ronnie said sharply, dismayed by her own tired irritability. "Ask Mr. von Hurst to please make sure I know this man's name before I greet him!"

If he was surprised by his mistress's uncharacteristic outburst, Henri gave no sign. As usual, he clicked his heels, bowed, and left her.

Ronnie finished her coffee and wandered out to the garden, pacifying herself with the selection of flowers. She loved the garden and had nurtured it with tender care, giving her flowers the affection she needed to release. And although she did the planning for any entertainment or renovation, the house actually ran smoothly without her. The black-and-tan coonhounds that roamed the estate were well looked after by the kennel keeper, and the four American saddle horses were tended by a conscientious groom. Only the flowers really depended on her, and so they received her devotion.

Now she savored their sweet aromas, wrinkling her nose into their blossoms as the softness of the petals caressed her cheeks. She clipped and pruned a colorful assortment, planning a myriad display for the huge formal dining table, which would be used that night. Then, with a streak of impishness, she planned an arrangement for their guest's room. If the man was hard as tacks, she mused, a little flower softness might be in order.

Returning to the house, Ronnie set to her arrangements, dryly appreciating the fact that they were to have company. She so desperately wanted to keep her mind busy! To worry about Pieter brought about useless pain; to think about her excursion into the arms of Drake brought agony. To tangle with them both brought a torturous guilt. In the eyes of the world she was married, and she had willingly sought out another man.

But her heart cried out that it was impossible to be untrue to a husband who had never been one with her. She vaguely wondered what her life might have been like had Jamie not senselessly lost his life to drugs. But that was all so long ago. It was in her extreme youth; it was the past. She could barely remember Jamie's face. When she tried to recall it, another appeared—that of Drake O'Hara. And she was back to self-incrimination. . . .

"Mrs. von Hurst?"

"Yes?" Ronnie glanced up as Henri stepped quietly into the salon where she continued to absently trim leaves from her flowers.

"You requested the name of your guest. He is Mister Drake O'Hara of Chicago, Illinois, owner and proprietor of the American International Galleries. Mr. von Hurst would like you to be aware that—Mrs. von Hurst! Are you quite all right, madam?"

Ronnie wasn't all right. The room was spinning around her, going completely black, and spinning around her again. Her heart had ceased to beat. She felt as if she had been drained of blood.

"Mrs. von Hurst!"

49

For once Henri dropped his cold dignity to rush to her side, appalled by the parchment-white color that had overtaken his usually healthy mistress. He caught her just as her slender body wavered and angled toward the floor.

Ronnie snapped back into physical control at Henri's touch, numb, but aware that she needed to be coherent. Blotting the panic out of her mind and wondering what cruel trick of fate could make such a thing happen, she forced herself to breathe and to find a voice to reply to Henri as she straightened from his saving hold.

"The sun, Henri, I think I stayed out to long. . . . Could you please . . . would you get me a glass of water?"

"Certainly, Mrs. von Hurst," Henri exclaimed, loathe to release her until she was seated. "Certainly . . . immediately. . . ." Watching her with concern, he hurried to carry out his errand.

Ronnie closed her eyes and kept breathing deeply, willing her heart to beat normally and her blood to pulse regularly through her veins. It wasn't possible. It simply wasn't possible. There had to be another Drake O'Hara.

And yet she knew there wasn't.

She had been destined to meet the man she had chosen wildly as a companion in a clandestine affair long before she had ever seen his intensely probing, magnetic, dark-brown eyes. . . .

He's coming here! she thought desperately, struck by another wave of panic. *Oh, God, oh no, oh no. . . .*

Henri walked quickly back into the room with a glass of cool water. Ronnie accepted it with a grateful smile and drained it in a moment. Smiling up at the butler, she thanked him.

"Perhaps I should call the doctor," Henri said doubtfully.

"No! Heavens, no!" Ronnie exclaimed hastily. "I'm fine. Really fine, I promise you. It was just the heat. And Henri—I would prefer it if we not mention this little spell of mine to Mr. von Hurst. I fear it might needlessly upset him."

"As you wish, madam."

Henri was quick to agree with her. He knew that there were

days when Pieter von Hurst totally ignored his wife, but he also knew that the temperamental artist would worry incessantly if he thought anything was wrong.

"Now"—Ronnie leaned back in her chair with a bright smile affixed to her face—"you were telling me about . . . er . . . this man. Drake O'Hara. Was there anything else Mr. von Hurst wanted me to know?"

She listened, registering facts without really hearing. O'Hara, a man who dabbled in sculpture himself, owned the most prestigious galleries in the Midwest. His shows were legendary; he could make or break an artist with a single critique.

It was shocking, really, that she hadn't known the name. But, she had been in Paris and then on a remote island for many years.

"Thank you, Henri," Ronnie told him placidly, hoping she could trust her legs to carry her. "I think I'll go up to my room and rest for a bit."

"Shall I have Gretel send you a luncheon tray?" Obviously Henri was still concerned.

Ronnie smiled wanly. "Yes, thank you, that would be nice. . . ."

She made it up the spiral staircase to her room, where she sat numbly at the foot of the bed.

In a matter of a few short hours she was going to have to stand in the doorway and greet a man as a total stranger who she already knew more thoroughly than any human being. . . .

They would be staying under the same roof for God only knew how long.

It was impossible! What was she going to do? How could she endure seeing him day after day?

And, dear God, what was going to happen when Drake saw her? His opinion of married women who carried on affairs had been blatant. He had loved her so fiercely, and now he scorned her with equal fervor. Would he deem it proper to tell Pieter?

A laugh of hysteria was rising in her throat. Pieter, in his present mood, might be pleased to discover she had taken a lover

51

... but certainly not amused to find that he had invited his wife's impetuous lover into his own home.

All she could do was pray that Drake showed no sign of recognition until she could talk to him alone and convince him that upsetting Pieter could be dangerous to his condition. Supposedly the great gallery owner was visiting Pieter because he admired and respected the great artist. Surely he would do nothing to harm such an illustrious idol.

Ronnie's slender fingers wound into tense fists, her nails tearing into her own flesh. She pounded against the mattress with venom and despair, striking the thick padding until she wore herself out.

It was impossible! she kept railing in whispered curses to whatever deity lurked above. Incredible, impossible.

But it was happening.

And somehow she was going to have to not only live through it but carry the entire thing off without the hint of a hitch. She couldn't afford the luxury of more tears or hysteria.

She had to prepare herself to walk down the staircase with all the effortless poise of the irreproachably elegant Mrs. Pieter von Hurst.

CHAPTER THREE

Ronnie had probably never taken more care to dress in her life. But her clothes that night would be like a knight's shield of heavy armor. They would protect her from searing dark eyes that could thrust daggers into her soul.

Her hair, clean and fragrantly scented, was piled on her head in burnished waves of gleaming sable. Delicate diamond earrings dangled from her earlobes, catching and reflecting the deep midnight blue of her silk cocktail sheath. Loathe to play the coward, she had chosen the backless dress on purpose, knowing it displayed the shapely contours Pieter found so fascinating for his sculpture.

At five o'clock she was standing beside her husband in the elegant entry hall, her hand resting lightly on Pieter's velvet-clad arm, evidencing none of the turmoil that raged through her.

Pieter looked well that night. Despite his gauntness, he was a tall man and, with the shoulders of his tailored suit well padded, he enhanced the illusion of a delicate form of health—one that befitted a dedicated artist.

Ronnie's hand tightened in an involuntary shudder as Henri opened the doors. It was the first time in their married life that she had leaned upon Pieter. But her face remained impassive. Even as Drake O'Hara moved into the hallway, towering in the shadow of the encroaching dusk, she stood immobile, a polite smile of greeting frozen on her placid face.

"Drake!" Pieter moved forward to shake the enthusiastically outstretched hand of the younger, more robust man, and Ronnie blinked once as she realized the two men had met at some previous time.

"Pieter," Drake returned, a smile warming the sinister male darkness of his angular features. "You're looking good, damn good."

It was then that his eyes flickered with glittering anticipation to Ronnie, and then froze, locked, and turned to pits of the deepest dark hell.

Ronnie wasn't breathing. She waited, too numb to pray.

But though his telltale eyes burned her heart to quaking cinders, Drake's face registered no change, unless it was a wry lift to one corner of his mustach-covered lip.

She, after all, had been prepared. He hadn't.

"Forgive me, Pieter, for staring," Drake said, his cool smile deepening for Pieter's benefit. "Your wife"—he inclined his head to Ronnie—"has an uncanny beauty."

"Ah, yes." Pieter was pleased by Drake's statement, noticing nothing amiss. "Come here, my dear, and meet a longtime friend and comrade, Drake O'Hara. Drake, my wife, Veronica."

It took every ounce of willpower Ronnie had to raise her hand and have it engulfed by Drake's powerful, punishing one. "Mr. O'Hara," she managed coolly, "welcome to our home."

"Thank you," he replied, refusing to lift his burning gaze from hers. "Please, call me Drake. I believe the circumstances warrant a first-name basis."

Smiling wanly, Ronnie delicately withdrew her hand, tugging slightly. He released her with a casual finesse.

"Pieter." Ronnie turned to her husband. "Shall we adjourn to the salon for drinks?" Damn, she needed a drink. She was grateful that Drake had seen fit to hold his silence, and mercifully control his recognition, but still, if she was to endure the condemnation in his hell-fire eyes, she needed a drink. Probably several.

"Yes, by all means." Pieter was actually sounding jovial. He clapped his hand upon Drake's back, his bony fingers ludicrous against the imposing breadth. "Come, my friend, it's been years. We have a lot of catching up to do."

Ronnie sailed ahead of the two men, listening vaguely to their chatter about Chicago, the state of the arts, and the Von Hursts' home on the island. In the comfortably tasteful salon she hurried to the small but well-stocked rosewood bar and slipped behind it, feeling absurdly that she had found another shield. Any distance between herself and Drake was beneficial. She knew his eyes followed her relentlessly; she could sense them as if they were tangible fires, and she refused to look into them.

"Drake, what can I get you?" she inquired, busily setting up glasses. She dropped ice into only two of them, knowing that when her husband drank, it was neat Scotch. He still abhorred the American custom of cold liquor.

"A bourbon, please, with a splash of soda," Drake replied politely. He leaned his vibrant form against the bar, forcing her to an awareness of the leashed energy that composed him. His fingers closed over hers again as she pushed his glass toward him, tightening momentarily and drawing from her a shiver of apprehension. From the corner of her eye she could see that he had felt the shiver, and that it had given him grave satisfaction. His lips were twisted into a dry, hard grin.

Ronnie mentally squared her shoulders. She couldn't allow him to believe he could intimidate her. Moving serenely from the bar without glancing his way, she brought the crystal rock glass of straight Scotch to Pieter and, carrying her own highball of Seagram's and Seven, chose an encompassing provincial chair apart from the others. The men seated themselves after her and immediately fell back into comfortable, reacquainting conversation. Sipping on the drink she had made much stronger than usual, Ronnie let their words float around her head, learning that her husband and Drake had met years before: once in Pieter's Dutch homeland, and once in Chicago. The first American showing of Pieter's work had been at Drake's galleries, hence Drake's determination now to push Pieter to greater productivity.

"You've been hiding out on this island too long," Drake told Pieter. He seemed perfectly at ease, one long leg crossed over the other at an angle, his hand resting on one knee. Ronnie was sure she had been temporarily forgotten, but then he turned to her. "Of course, that's perfectly understandable. Had I your lovely wife, I might be tempted to spirit her away to an island myself."

It was a perfectly innocent compliment. Only Ronnie understood the undertones. *Keep her safely away from all others.*

Pieter was pleased as always when reference was made to his wife's beauty. He chuckled quietly, and, at another time, Ronnie would have been equally pleased to see the happiness that was easing the terrible strain of his pinched features. "Ronnie and I find great pleasure in our island. We seldom leave it."

"Ah," Drake inferred with a teasing tone, "but you must sometimes!"

Ronnie unfurled from her chair and rose gracefully to her feet. "I believe I shall fix myself another drink," she said smoothly, ignoring Drake's comment. "How about you, gentlemen?"

Pieter declined, but Drake grinned at her cruelly. "Please."

As hostess she had no choice but to walk to him and retrieve his empty glass. And at that moment she hated him intensely. It was obvious that her wishful assessment had been correct; Drake admired Pieter and would say or do nothing to hurt him.

But he didn't intend to let her forget a thing. It was evident that he was barely concealing his disdain, evident that he believed whatever torture he inflicted upon her was more than warranted.

Taking Drake's glass as swiftly as was conceivably polite, Ronnie met his gaze for an instant of open hostility, determined not to wilt before his fire. She spun away from him and retreated once more to the bar, grateful for the mechanical tasks that kept her moving with the natural autonomy of a brilliantly programmed robot.

She was also grateful for the years that had bred self-restraint. If she had had to depend on instinct, she would have run screaming into the night, hands clenched tightly to her head to drown out the clamoring emotions that pierced through the numbness that had claimed her.

Her heart bled for Pieter. And she hated Drake. Hated him for judging without knowing . . . hated him with even more vehemence, because she knew that by all outward appearances he had come to the only possible conclusions. . . .

Yet she hated him mostly because of her own sense of bewilderment and shame. When he looked at her, when his hands grazed over hers, when she inhaled the too-familiar drugging scent that exuded from his coiled frame, she wanted him again. Sensitivities that had lain dormant all those years had been reawakened by this man who now despised her, but God help her, despite his scorn, despite her honest but different love for Pieter, she couldn't stop her tormented mind from bringing her back to those cherished hours of curling against his magnificent naked form. . . .

Ronnie didn't attempt to meet Drake's eyes as she returned his fresh drink and once more took her chair. The conversation turned to the quality of various marble, and she found herself speaking occasionally, her tone deadened, but all her inflections in the right place.

This time her drink was almost straight Seagram's. She welcomed the choking heat that burned down her throat, blazing much-needed bravado through her system.

After dinner, she was going to lock herself in her room and get rip-roaring drunk. The next day's hangover would be a small price to pay for that night's solace.

Henri made one of his proper entrances to announce that dinner was served. Pieter and Drake both sprang to their feet to escort her graciously into the formal dining room. Despite the warmth of the liquor, Drake's touch on her arm was as hot as a branding iron; his sardonic grin as he towered above her as cutting as an unsheathed foil.

It was impossible for her to do anything more than pick at the excellent meal of stuffed grouse that she had planned for the evening. The crystals of the multifaceted chandelier swam together above her head, fogging the brilliant colors of the flowers she had cut with such complacency earlier in the day.

"Certainly," she suddenly heard Drake saying dryly. "A gem above all others."

Ronnie's eyes rose from absent concentration on her plate to glance quickly from man to man. They had been discussing her openly, and she hadn't heard a word that was said.

"An amazing talent," Drake continued, raising his wineglass a hair as he steadily returned her inadvertent glance. "Uniquely stunning; the most charming chatelaine. I'm sure all of her . . . ah . . . talents, are equally pleasing."

There was no way to prevent the rush of crimson that stained her face in a wild flush of fury. How could he be so insinuative with Pieter at the same table?

Because Pieter was blissfully unaware. The comment meant nothing to him. Only Ronnie knew the degrading implication. . . .

"Ronnie excels at nothing so well as being my model," Pieter was saying cheerfully, oblivious to the color of his wife's face as he studiously cut his food. "But you'll see what I mean tomorrow."

"What?" The squeaked question was out before Ronnie realized she had voiced it.

Pieter finally looked up, frowning. "I told you, Ronnie, Drake is also a sculptor. I intend to draw him into our work." His brooding gaze left her to travel to Drake with a hint of pride. "This young man could probably have far surpassed me in genius if his interests weren't so diversified. His hands war with his mind—art and business. But he has come to push *me*. I intend to push in return and involve him in our project."

Ronnie placed her fork down and reached for her water glass, dismayed by the trembling that assailed her fingers. She couldn't possibly model with Drake in the room. Pieter was carving the curves of her back into pink marble. Sitting for her husband was clinical. Sitting, clothed only in drapery, while the two chiseled

58

and discussed human anatomy, using her like the marble beneath their hands, would be enough to drive her over the brink.

She would be like a fish out of water, exposed, totally vulnerable to whatever verbal attack Drake chose to make.

And he knew it. He raised his glass higher to her as a single brow quirked high in cynical amusement. "I shall be looking forward to tomorrow."

Ronnie drained the entire glass of water, only to find that the effort still did nothing to dampen her desert-dry throat.

There could be no tomorrow. She was determined and adamant. But now was not the time to argue with Pieter. They did not argue, or even "discuss," in front of others, but this was one time she would make an unrelenting stand against the man she strove to please in all other ways.

Drake must have sensed her plan to protest. "Please don't be distressed, Veronica," he told her glibly. "I assure you that I am a legitimate artist."

Pieter waved his hand in the air with dramatic dismissal. "Don't worry about Ronnie, Drake. She's a very professional lady."

"And one who needs a bit of air," Ronnie declared, unable to sit still any longer and be discussed as if she weren't present. Rising quickly, she murmured, "If you'll excuse me for a moment . . ."

Pieter might be shocked that she was walking out on company, but that too would have to be brought up later. She was getting out of the room.

Both men rose quickly. "Certainly, my dear," Pieter murmured in response, concern in his tone. But there was also anger. Ronnie didn't really care. Maybe it was time she stopped catering to him.

"I'll rejoin you shortly," she promised, surprised by the cool determination of her own voice, "back in the salon for brandy. . . ."

She was sailing regally out the door before either man could give further contemplation to her abrupt departure.

But she wasn't out of earshot quickly enough to miss Pieter's damning words as the two reseated themselves.

"I doubt if Veronica will be modeling much longer for me, which means my project must be completed soon. Her loyalty to me has been excessive, but I'd like to see her pursuing a few new interests. . . ."

She was going to scream. Either that or bury herself beneath the fertile soil that harbored her cherished plants. . . .

But she did neither. She did flee to the garden, discarding her stately walk as soon as she had left the house behind. Her heels twisted in the dirt as she ran, wrenching her ankles, but she didn't care. She needed time desperately. Time to retrieve a measure of dignity.

She was panting when she reached the little tile paths that ran among her flowers and the fountains that played in the garden. Finding the wrought iron love seat wedged near the rear wall, she sank onto it, automatically straightening the tendrils of sleek auburn hair that had fallen loose in her reckless run.

Now, more than ever, she had to talk to Drake alone. Without giving away any of the truth, she had to somehow subtly convince this man who had torn into her life like a cyclone that he could endanger her husband's precarious health.

She never heard his footsteps. He came upon her as silently as a wraith, a shocking feat for a man of his size and robust vitality. Her first knowledge that he had come upon her was the result of his raw words.

"So—the 'Mrs.' that doesn't matter is Von Hurst. Tacky, madam. That name has mattered with incredible importance for almost twenty years."

"What are you doing out here?" Ronnie bit back sharply. She didn't need to feign civility out there.

"Pieter is concerned," Drake drawled mockingly, setting a polished shoe upon the love seat, his hands in his pockets, leaning toward her. "The poor man doesn't seem to know what's gotten into his precious wife. Actually, it seems there's a lot the poor man doesn't know about his wife."

Ronnie curled her nails into the iron pattern of the seat, wishing fervently that she could flail them across his hard, accusing, bronze face and draw the blood he seemed to want from her.

The metal grating beneath her fingers braced her with the illusion of strength. She lifted her chin high and forced her eyes to brazen into his. She clenched her teeth together, then parted them to speak with a collected firmness.

"And do you intend to inform Pieter that you have been previously acquainted with his wife?"

Dark eyes swept her contemptuously from head to toe. "I shouldn't answer that. I should let you worry." He planted his foot back on the ground, dusted the love seat, flung back his jacket tails, and sat beside her. Unwittingly Ronnie found herself shrinking as far to the side as the seat would allow.

"My, my, what are we afraid of?" Drake mocked grimly, catching her wrist with a coiled menace. "My touch? Ahhh, but there was a time when you begged for it, Mrs. von Hurst."

"Please!" Ronnie murmured, twisting her wrist within his crushing grip as her teeth sank into her lip.

"A note of distress? I'm truly touched!" His teeth flashed in a wicked grin as he brought his face menacingly close to hers. Again she thought that his eyes were like a black fire, capable of burning flesh with all the true heat of hell.

"Drake, please," she protested, wincing. He was so close that his mustache tickled the peach softness of her skin, tantalizing her, terrifying her. "Pieter is right inside—"

With a curt laugh he withdrew and dropped her hand as if it were poison. "You needn't fear advances from me, Mrs. von Hurst," he grated, his tone dripping the venom of his eyes. Apparently his mind was running along the same lines as hers. "My dear, sweet poison beauty. I happen to think the world of Pieter von Hurst. I wouldn't think of touching his wife. It was a vast pity I ever did."

Ronnie had to find a way to fight her tears and ignore his cutting cynicism.

"So you don't intend to say anything to Pieter?" she inquired flatly, unconsciously rubbing her wrist as she stared into the foliage before her.

"No, I don't. I see no reason to hurt the man. He has obviously been gravely ill."

Ronnie breathed a silent sigh of relief. "Thank you," she said stiffly.

"Don't thank me!" His hiss was soft, but to her ears it came as a roar. "I'm not doing anything for you. It's my sound opinion that you should be horsewhipped. My God, woman! Your heart must be chiseled out of marble! Running around on a man who has given you his adoration on a platter, a man who has been ill. A man like Pieter von Hurst!" His voice rang with his own self-disgust for having had the affair, and Ronnie inwardly cringed.

"I don't have to listen to your judgments," she said hollowly.

"Wrong, Mrs. von Hurst," Drake said, a gravel-like tone lacing his voice.

Ronnie tensed, aware of the extent of his anger, acutely sensing the depth of the coiled strength that breathed beside her, held in check by sheer willpower. She didn't dare breathe, or make a move herself, when he again picked up her hand, idly trailing his tanned fingers over the faint blue veins.

"I'm afraid, Ronnie, that you'll have to listen to every word I have to say—until I leave, that is, which could be awhile yet—because there is one thing that could make me tell Pieter about his precious wife."

"Oh?" Ronnie heard her own voice, coming with faint curiosity, as if it were very far away. "And what is that?"

"Well," Drake said, matter-of-factly, "the slightest implication that your excessive loyalty has turned to a few new interests."

Ronnie involuntarily attempted to snatch her hand away, but Drake held it securely. She tried to turn her head completely from his, but he caught her chin with his other hand and held it firmly, lowering his own autocratic features over hers again. "Let's not play this too cool, shall we, Mrs. von Hurst?" he lashed out icily. "I don't know what your personal game is, but I do hope you know what you're doing. Potential consequences, you know. Say, should you produce a child, I can guarantee you I'll be back—to claim it."

Ronnie gasped, shocked by his vehemence and firm determination, and the very idea. "There is no child," she rasped, adding with narrowed eyes. "And you couldn't."

"Try me."

"It's irrelevant," she grated, swallowing. "Pieter—"

"I'm afraid Pieter would have to discover at that point that his wife is a crystal angel with the devil's own heart."

"Don't worry, at that point—" Ronnie began desperately. She broke off her own words. To go further would be to betray the confidence Pieter had entrusted her with. "Could you please let go of my chin?" she demanded haughtily.

He shook his head relentlessly. "I want to stare into those beautiful blue eyes when I listen to your treachery."

Ronnie grated her teeth with fury, further irked because she feared she would soon start trembling. It was too easy to remember when those same dark eyes had stared into hers with tenderness, too easy to remember when his touch was gentle, tender, demanding nothing but that she love him with equal ardency. . . .

"Drake, please"—she searched his eyes for a shred of compassion and found none—"I swear to you. There is no child."

"And how do you know?" he queried sceptically, reminding her that forty-eight hours hadn't passed since they'd parted.

"Believe me, I know," she said with all the confidence she could muster. "I—" She faltered only a second. "I do know what I'm doing. This is the nineteen eighties."

He released her chin and hand and stood, annoying her as he towered above her. "Well, I don't know," he informed her curtly. "And I promise you, I'll be waiting to see. I'd hate to hazard a guess about you and Pieter, but the time you spent with me was wildly potent. You were a wanton. . . ."

Ronnie sprang to her feet, wilder than Drake had ever seen

63

her, any semblance of her regal cool shot entirely to the winds of mindless wrath. She didn't give a damn at that moment if her house guest reappeared inside with her hand print clearly etched on the side of his face.

But she never raised her hand. His arms locked around her body as soon as as she sprang up. "No, no, no, Mrs. von Hurst. No outraged violence. I won't tolerate it from a woman who literally asked me to take her."

Seething with frustration, Ronnie went limp. To pinnacle her wretchedness the shelter of his arms, even in anger, was dangerously enticing. She so desperately wanted to bury her head in the mass of hair that she knew lurked beneath the crisp tie and pressed dress shirt; so desperately wanted to blurt out everything that had happened, the way that everything was. . . .

She stiffened her slender spine and met his eyes. Exhausted, dejected, she spoke to him tiredly. "I think we'd better get in. Pieter might start worrying."

He let her go and, squaring her shoulders, she started back down the tile path.

"Ronnie."

She stopped and turned back without expression as he called her name.

"You will sit tomorrow."

She shrugged dispiritedly. Arguing with Pieter could have caused him a lapse anyway, and he was looking so happy.

"Yes, I'll sit," she said coldly, resuming her trip back to the house.

Drake watched her go in a torn agony himself. He didn't know what to think, but he couldn't help what he felt.

Logically she was poison. A cold-hearted temptress. A woman who would betray an ailing husband to partake in an illicit affair with all-out ardency, and, unwittingly, granted, use against that husband a man who was his most fervent fan.

Used. Drake knew he had been used more shockingly than ever, and it was that thought that fully boiled his blood to where the cap could barely be kept on his steaming temper.

But it was impossible to look at her and not be touched, not be swept back into a land of passion and tenderness.

She was still incredibly beautiful. And majestic. That proud lift of her shoulders and bracing of her spine when challenged . . .

She would never be cornered.

And then there were those eyes. Those beautiful blue eyes that had been haunting him since he first saw her. Eyes that could freeze with blue ice. Cold, assured, confident eyes, which every once in a rare while relented and lost their guard.

And then they could be beseechingly, trustingly warm—the eyes of a sensitive, sensuous woman. Eyes that lured him into a silken trap, made him fantasize . . . made him believe against all reason that she was all things good—love, devotion, and loyalty. . . .

But that was ridiculous—she was none of those things. And if his haunted body still yearned for her with an alien singleness and treachery, it didn't matter.

He could never touch her again.

She was Von Hurst's wife.

CHAPTER FOUR

As Ronnie hurried along the path she heard her name called again. Stopping, she saw that Drake was catching up with her, his long strides bringing him quickly along.

"Don't you think we should make an appearance together?" he suggested mildly, his expression now fathomless. "I was sent to escort you back in."

Ronnie watched him contemplatively for several seconds, then her dark lashes swept over her cheeks. "I suppose," she said indifferently.

He offered her his arm, and she accepted it lightly as they returned to the house. Pieter was already in the salon, where Henri was preparing stout snifters of a fine cognac.

"Ah—there you are!" Pieter greeted them jovially. His gaze alighted upon his wife with mild curiosity. "Are you quite all right, my dear?"

"Yes, fine." Ronnie smiled weakly, accepting her cognac with a nod of thanks to Henri. "I've a bit of a headache, though." She kept her gaze upon Pieter rather than Drake. "If you two will forgive me, I think I'll excuse myself shortly and retire for the night."

Pieter frowned and nodded his acquiescence. "My wife, I'm afraid, Drake, will need her rest. I don't go about much myself these days, so she'll be your escort around the island." His frown deepened and his brooding eyes turned to probe Ronnie. "I hope you didn't acquire sunstroke aboard that ship. Too much time in the sun is not healthy."

66

Ronnie tensed, sipping on her cognac. She didn't dare look in Drake's direction. "I'm fine, Pieter, just a little tired. I—er—I really wasn't in the sun that much." She winced at the folly of her last statement. If she had ever left an opening for Drake to pounce upon, that was it. But he said nothing. She couldn't see him from the angle of her chair, but she could sense his presence as he casually leaned against the bar.

Pieter turned to him in explanation. "Ronnie just sailed off on one of those Harbor cruises you see advertised." He lifted a gaunt hand in the air. "As I've said, I seldom leave the house myself. Veronica, however, is still young. I insist that she occasionally get out and enjoy herself."

"How nice," Drake replied, his tone betraying nothing. Ronnie could feel his dark eyes turn to her. "And did you enjoy yourself, Mrs. von Hurst? I hear that those cruises can be very pleasant—offering every amenity."

"Thank you, yes," Ronnie replied coolly, rising, still refusing to glance his way. "I did enjoy the cruise. Pieter"—she moved swiftly to her husband to drop a quick kiss on top of his thinning blond head, certain he would not brush her aside with company in the room—"I'm going up, if you don't mind. Mr. O'Hara"— she finally lifted her eyes to Drake's with a daring shade of defiance—"I do hope you'll forgive me. However, I'm sure that you and my husband have a multitude of things to discuss." With the regality of a queen, Ronnie then sailed from the room with her head high.

"I wonder," she heard Pieter murmuring absently as she closed the salon doors behind her, "if I'm fair to Ronnie in many ways. . . ."

Ronnie grimaced as she started up the spiral stairway. Pieter couldn't know it, but his statement had probably given his guest quite a laugh.

The headache she had invented was pounding away in her skull as she reached the sanctuary of her room. Rubbing her temple assiduously, she kicked off her shoes and haphazardly began shedding her clothes, heedless for once of where things fell. She lay in her bed, clad only in her lace bra and panties, fighting the waves of nausea that assailed her and simultaneously discarding her idea to drink herself into oblivion.

The highballs, wine, and cognac she had already drunk hadn't done a thing to improve the situation, they had only added physical torture to mental! If she just lay still, very, very still . . .

Somewhere along the line she must have dozed off. She awoke with a start—and the immediate tingling, uncanny perception that she was not alone in the room. A scream rose in her throat, but before she could give vent to the sound a hand clamped tightly over her mouth. She knew instantly the scent and touch of the hand, as she did the deep voice that hissed, "Hush, it's me."

Shivering with both outrage and fear, Ronnie pushed at his hand and struggled into a sitting position, meeting his sinister dark gaze in the light of the moon with her own eyes snapping sapphire glints. "What are you doing in here!" she hissed furiously in return, wishing she had thought to draw down the covers before she had plopped on the bed. Her instinct was to grab something to clutch to herself, but there was nothing available.

"I haven't come to assault your dubious virtue," he commented dryly, his hips perched beside hers on the bed. "I want to know what's wrong with Pieter."

Ronnie's lashes fell, but she was quick with a comeback. "I think you could have found a better time to discuss Pieter!"

"Oddly enough, my dear Mrs. von Hurst, this seems to be the only time I can guarantee having an audience with you alone."

Ronnie blinked rapidly, highly aware of her state of undress, whether he was or not. Apparently he already knew beyond a doubt that she and Pieter did not share a room.

"Pieter has not been well," she said quickly.

"Obviously," Drake drawled. His arms on either side of her, not touching her, held her as if between bars. His dark face, ruggedly swarthy in the moonlight, moved within inches of her own. "What's wrong with him?" It was a demand, not a question.

Ronnie clenched her teeth, meeting his stare silently as she played for time to think of an appropriate answer. His gaze momentarily left her face to sweep over her form and the cream of her silky skin displayed enticingly by the expensively cut underwear. Chills as vibrant as tiny electrical shocks seemed to prick at Ronnie's flesh, but his gaze returned to hers, cold and disinterested. "Well?"

"Drake," she began haughtily, "I'd appreciate it if you left my room. My husband—"

"Your husband isn't coming anywhere near here, and you and I both know it," Drake cut in coldly. "How long has Pieter been ill?"

"If you're concerned for Pieter, you'll get out," Ronnie retorted.

"I'll be happy to leave," Drake promised sardonically, "as soon as you answer my questions."

Ronnie blinked again, then released an exasperated sigh. She couldn't tell him anything, but she had to get him away from her. Her outrage was fast losing its intensity; the temptation to reach out and touch his harshly squared jaw was seeping through her to obliterate reason.

"I cannot discuss my husband's condition," she said flatly, fixing her vision upon his jacket sleeve. "Yes, as you have so brilliantly observed, Pieter has been ill. If you wish further answers, you'll have to ask him."

"Why?"

"Why?" Ronnie ejaculated, her voice rising with desperate annoyance at his persistence. "Because I have given Pieter my oath not to discuss him with anyone!"

"It would seem you have given him other oaths that you have seen fit to break," Drake grated harshly, pulling from her, his hand trailing a path insinuatingly across her midriff as he did so.

"Please, Drake," Ronnie begged, lowering her voice again with acute misery. "This is Pieter's house."

"I see—the place makes a difference."

"You wouldn't understand."

"I understand too well."

"Drake—"

"Don't fret, Mrs. von Hurst. I wouldn't touch you with a ten-foot pole." He stood abruptly, making her feel far worse and even more vulnerable as he towered above her, his broad shoulders rigid. "Is Pieter under a doctor's care?"

"Yes," Ronnie whispered, snatching her pillow from behind her back to clench over her torso. "The best."

Drake spun on his heels and quietly padded across the room to the door. He paused for only a second, his hand on the knob. In the darkness she could still see the burning glitter of his dark eyes. "Don't be a hypocrite, Ronnie. The pillow bit was definitely unnecessary. There isn't an inch of you I don't know better than the back of my own hand." His gaze raked over her one last time, fathomlessly. "See you tomorrow."

Then he was gone, and she was left to lie awake for the rest of the night, alternately feeling as if she were as hot as lava and then as frigidly frozen as a bleak stretch of Antarctic ice.

By morning Ronnie's nerves were sadly on edge. She was grateful when she dressed and cautiously walked downstairs to find herself alone in the dining room. There was no evidence that Drake and Pieter had eaten and left, but then she didn't expect to find any. Henri would have removed an empty coffee cup before the china had time to grow cold.

Intuitively certain that she would have a respite of peace, Ronnie decided she was famished. Making up for the meals she had barely touched, she piled her plate high with the cheese blintzes that were Gretel's specialty, lavishing them with thick mounds of strawberry jam and sour cream. She also prowled through the remaining chafing dishes, adding to her plate crisp slices of bacon, smoked Virginia ham, and a spoonful of the grits that Pieter considered "animal mash" but consistently ordered for the morning buffet. It was one of the small courtesies his continental mind tolerated for his born-and-bred southern wife;

70

one of the little niceties that tugged at Ronnie's heart. No matter how bitter, withdrawn, and cruel Pieter had been at times, she knew he never intentionally used her as a scapegoat. Remembering the little things, the trivial things like grits, was Pieter's way of apologizing, of telling her that he did appreciate all that she did, the untiring devotion she gave to him.

Because, despite the fact that Pieter seldom allowed her near him, and often exploded against her when she was, she had allowed him to keep the two things a desperately ill man needed most fervently: his dignity and pride.

Reflecting on Pieter now, Ronnie wondered if she would have actually married him had he not become so sick. With Pieter, she had always responded to respect, ardor, and compassion *with* respect, ardor, and compassion. Her brief, shining love for Jamie had been very different. They had both been young Americans finding the wings of adulthood and romance in the spirited streets of Paris. They were both explorers, adventurers. They fought with a verbal vengeance, and patched up their quarrels with tears and passion.

She could honestly say that she had loved Jamie. And Pieter had a part of her heart that he would hold forever. Yet neither began to compare with the intensity of emotion she felt for Drake. His touch stirred senses she hadn't known existed; the mere sight or sound of him sent her mind reeling. But it was more than a physical draw. During that one day that now played havoc upon her world in memory, she had come to love him for the man he was, for the honesty of his word and his actions, for the tenderness only a man of his character could freely display. . . .

Damn it! she thought with annoyance. It wasn't safe to think about anything anymore! All roads led to Drake O'Hara.

"Goodness, woman! How the hell do you stay so thin eating like that?"

Ronnie's eyes flew to the doorway, where Drake stood, dressed in a casual short-sleeved shirt and black pants, one hand stuck in a pocket, the other bracing his frame as he lightly leaned against oak paneling. His lips were curled in a half-smile that tilted his mustache to a rakish angle, making the harsh contours of his face devilishly charming.

She wondered if the look was a form of peace treaty. He acted as if they had never exchanged words—or anything else for that matter.

Determined not to be the one to cast oil upon still waters, Ronnie answered him with the polite truth. "I don't usually get quite this carried away."

Drake smiled in return and walked to the buffet to pour himself a cup of coffee. Lifting the silver pot, he arched a brow to her. "Can I refill your cup?"

"Please." Ronnie pushed her coffee cup forward and watched as the dark liquid rose in a cloud of steam. She added cream and sugar to her coffee as Drake sat in the chair beside hers.

"This is a beautiful place," Drake commented.

"Thank you."

"Where are you really from?"

Ronnie shot him a wary glance, but the question was straightforward. At her look his lips curled even further, lightening his eyes. "I mean, you are from the South."

Slightly amused by her own rush to be defensive, Ronnie suppressed a full-scale grin and nodded. "Durham, North Carolina."

"Did Pieter choose Charleston for you?"

"No," Ronnie told him, glad for the comfortable normalcy of their conversation. "He owned this place long before I met him. I believe he bought it on his first trip to the States."

"Well," Drake mused, idly stirring his spoon in his coffee, "you fit it well. But then you also—" He stopped, and Ronnie bit her lip. His first nontaunting compliment had been unintentionally marred. She was sure he had been about to say that she had also looked well upon the cruise ship.

Not wanting to let the easy repartee that had come between them dissipate, Ronnie ignored the abrupt end of his statement.

She lifted her cup and sipped her coffee musingly. "I've never been to Chicago. What is it like?"

"New York"—Drake grinned—"except that it's Chicago."

Ronnie laughed, and Drake went on to describe the city, extolling the virtues of the midwestern metropolis, but also giving a blunt appraisal of the problems and drawbacks. "It's a good city for artists," he ended. "The community supports the theater and the visual arts."

Ronnie chewed thoughtfully on a last piece of cheese blintz. "Charleston is much smaller, but I would say it's a supportive community." She found herself talking about the charm of southern living, unaware that she became more and more animated as she spoke, and beautifully charming. Drake again found himself fascinated by her voice and her every movement. She was such a complex creature. So cold with that tragic reserve, part warm with a wealth of spirit and vitality. He began to forget his reason for seeking her out.

"Ah, I've found you both!" Pieter broke in from the doorway. "Ready?"

"Yes, I am!" Drake declared, rising and moving to Ronnie to pull back her chair. "Ronnie?"

She glanced to her husband with a hint of confusion.

"The sitting," Pieter explained with a hint of exasperation. "I'd like to work now. The afternoons drain me, I'm afraid."

"Oh," Ronnie murmured uneasily. She rose and followed Pieter with no further comment, her spine straight, her shoulders squared. She knew now why Drake had called his unspoken truce and she wasn't sure whether to be grateful or suspicious. He had known the idea of posing before him and Pieter had disturbed her, and he had tried to ease the situation. But had it been an act of kindness, or was it self-beneficial?

It really didn't matter. An hour later Ronnie had already endured the misery she had expected, and had withdrawn from it, setting her mind as far away as possible. She was posed upon a settee, holding her position exactly as she had been long and laboriously trained to do. A single movement could send Pieter into a tirade.

Stiff muscles meant nothing to him in his pursuit of art. When she modeled, Ronnie knew, she lost her identity completely. She was nothing more than a tool to Pieter. He would set her up with fingers of ice and bark commands until she was perfect in his mind's eye.

Today had been worse than usual.

She was actually clad with a fair amount of respectability. She held her drapery high over her breasts, and Pieter had tucked it securely over her legs. Only her back was visible, but it was a visibility that would inherently make one nervous. To turn one's back on anyone for any length of time was to feel uncomfortably vulnerable. Especially when that back was the topic of conversation. Pieter was instructing Drake in planes and angles and curves. Clinically. She might have been an inanimate object . . . and certainly not his wife.

All her reserves of inner strength were called upon as Pieter asked Drake to learn by sense of touch. And she had to wonder sickly as she stared straight ahead, not breathing, blinking, or daring to move an eye covertly what Drake was thinking and feeling as his hands moved over her back, their touch fire to Pieter's ice. . . . She was amazed that her body followed the strict dictates of her mind, and that she neither flinched nor constricted into a mass of helpless quivers.

But finally, after vaguely listening to two hours worth of discussion on her own contours and the virtues of Venetian pink marble, Pieter let out a drawn sigh. "I believe I've pushed a bit too far. We'll quit for the day."

A haze of grateful tears welled in Ronnie's eyes to be instantly flicked away. She fought the urge to gather her drapery and shoot from the room like a bat out of hell and rose gracefully instead, calmly heading for the door. She even risked a cool glance in Drake's direction, but his eyes were on the tools he was carefully cleaning. Thank God for small favors. . . .

* * *

74

By the end of the week, however, Ronnie had learned to be grateful for Drake's presence in the studio. She had sneezed once, and Pieter's chisel had gone flying across the room. Drake's shocked stare had brought Pieter to the instant contrition he normally wouldn't have found for hours.

The entire house seemed to breathe new life with Drake in it. Although Ronnie was careful never to see him alone, she began to look forward to mealtimes, when she knew she would see him. Since the moments they had shared at the breakfast table on the day after his arrival, he had made every effort to be constantly cordial, if distant. And now that the initial shock of his arrival had subsided, Ronnie had regained the composure to act the collected hostess of her training and old-time southern background. She learned a new discipline, one that allowed her to be remotely yet perfectly polite while still enjoying the sight and sound of Drake's lean body and the mellow twang of his deep voice when he spoke.

The nights were still hell. She couldn't forget the fact that he slept just down the hall, and her body would burn as she tossed and turned, engulfed with longing, yet awash with shame. Sometimes when she finally slept, she would awaken again with a start, and she knew that she expected—and hoped—Drake had entered the room. And it was so stupid, because she also knew he would never enter again, and that if he did, it would be senseless. He wanted no further part of her; he had made that clear. And even if he did want her, she couldn't want him. . . .

It was a pity that the existence she had learned to tolerate with complacency had been so completely shattered.

Pieter cut the session extremely short on Friday morning. Startled, Ronnie took an uneasy look at her husband.

His skin had turned a terrible gray pallor; his hands, when he did not hold them behind his back, trembled with palsy. The health he had been clinging to since Drake's arrival was surely draining from him, and Ronnie knew he was hanging on to his last reserves of strength until he could be alone. He would not want Drake to see him feeble and in the chair.

Knowing her husband, Ronnie began to excuse herself, tallying an account of the things she had to do.

"Forget it, Ronnie." Pieter waved aside her plans. "We've offered Drake so little! I'd like you to take him for a ride around the island today. He's an expert horseman—I'm sure you'll find him up to our most rugged paths."

Ronnie had no doubt that Drake would be an expert horseman; she bitterly decided he would be an expert at anything he chose to do. But she couldn't think of a more trying afternoon than being alone in his company.

"Pieter, perhaps I should be here," she began tentatively.

"For what?" he demanded, his voice sharp. He couldn't tolerate a statement that he might need her.

"It's up to you, Ronnie," Drake interjected smoothly, intuitively stopping a battle before it could begin. His dark devillike eyes looked into hers with the briefest glint of understanding. "I would very much enjoy a good look at the island, but if you do have plans—"

"Nonsense," Pieter declared. "Ronnie has no plans that cannot wait."

"Ronnie?" Drake persisted.

"I'll be happy to accompany you for a ride around the island," Ronnie said uneasily, covertly watching Pieter. She would have promised anyone a ride in a spaceship to ease the tension and the sunken grayness of Pieter's skin, which was increasing by the second. "I'll, uh, need about fifteen minutes. I'll meet you by the stables."

"Fine," Drake agreed, his face troubled, his eyes on Pieter.

But Pieter was watching neither of them. He was attentively studying the work Drake had done for the day. Realizing he was being watched by them both, he looked up with a short laugh. "That's amazing . . ." he murmured, his hands moving reverently over the marble.

"Oh? What's that?" Drake queried, striding to join Pieter and glance down at his own creation with a puzzled frown.

"Those dimples," Pieter muttered. His eyes were still downcast over the marble, so neither Ronnie nor Drake saw the pensive speculation that lurked within them. "Those dimples beneath the spine . . . you've captured them in a stunning essence, and I hadn't even realized the draping was that low."

Ronnie stood dead still, hoping Pieter hadn't heard the horrible rasping of her indrawn breath, and hoping that Drake would answer suavely. . . .

He did. There wasn't a fraction of a second's hesitation before he smoothly chuckled in return. "The draping *wasn't* that low. I was taking a little artistic license, I'm afraid." His expression became suitably sheepish. "I suppose I haven't reached the point where artistic license is in order, but the chisel just seemed to go that way."

"No, no," Pieter protested, "you have done excellent work. The intuition was marvelous. I think you are wasting your time in the business side of the field."

"Thank you," Drake said quietly.

Ronnie sprang into action. "I'll go change," she murmured swiftly, gliding to the door. Turning for a moment of uncertainty, she kept her eyes blank and unwavering. "Pieter, shall I get you anything first?"

"No," Pieter returned abruptly. "Send Henri to me. Then please do not disturb me. I wish to be alone for the day."

Ronnie slid out the door, nodding. He was being rude, as was usually the case when he had his bad bouts, but he wasn't angry. Nor did he seem upset. Apparently he had accepted Drake's knowledge of her anatomy as imagination. As she closed the door she could still hear him speaking with Drake and, if anything, his tone was warmer and more cordial than before.

Pieter's thinking, however, involved more than mere suspicion. He had been watching Drake and Ronnie all week, and today had been the final assurance. He had known Ronnie was in love with Drake shortly after Drake's arrival. She wasn't in any way obvious, but Pieter could remember the way she had looked before Jamie died. That marvelous sparkle of sapphire in her eyes was a giveaway probably only he could fathom. Today he had learned for sure that Drake loved his wife. No, not his wife. He had to stop thinking of her with that title. Somehow he had to force himself to make the break before he could expect her to.

The two had been lovers at some time, Pieter knew. Fate, or coincidence, Drake must have been aboard the cruise. It hurt, he admitted. It hurt badly. And yet he was touched and flattered. Ronnie did care for him deeply. Even with the love that people spent their lives dreaming about within reach, she was refusing to leave him. And he knew the two of them were never intimate in his house.

It was also strangely palatable to lose her to a man like Drake. A lesser man would never have done. His ego wouldn't have tolerated it; there were times when his pride now went raw.

The knuckles in Pieter's bony hands cracked, and he realized how tightly he was clenching his fists. It was time he let her loose. She had never been his, just a loan from compassionate powers. She had given him the strength he now needed. But she was a tigress. Pairing her with a black panther was going to be tricky business, and he would still have to watch himself, because it did hurt.

Once in her room, Ronnie chose to wear her fawn-colored riding habit rather than jeans and a shirt, which she would have preferred. The habit was formal; jeans were not. Formality and distance were essential when she spent time with Drake.

With her hair in a neat knot and her riding cap in place, she zipped up her high black boots, sought out Henri to send for Pieter, and hurried out to the stables to have the horses saddled. Ronnie's mare, Scheherazade, was a gently spirited bay. Sure that Drake was the equestrian of Pieter's compliment, she chose Black Satan, a seventeen-hand magnificent stallion who lived up to his name, to be saddled for him. The two, she decided, matched one another. They were both the devil's own.

There was also a streak of mischief in her choice. Drake would be very busy handling the independent stallion, so busy, he couldn't possibly plague her with questions.

Drake appeared just as the groom was leading the horses to the mounting block. He watched Black Satan prance and snort and toss his well-defined head, then turned to Ronnie with an arched brow and a glint of amusement in his dark eyes.

"Is this an attempt at entertainment"—he chuckled—"or have you determined I have overstayed my welcome on your island? Am I supposed to be cast from the cliffs to the sea?"

Ronnie pursed her lips enigmatically. "I wouldn't think of offering you anything but our finest mount." Spinning in a smart circle, she sprang onto Scheherazade with practiced ease.

Drake shrugged and repeated her action with equal finesse, not losing a shred of confidence as the sleek black horse attempted to sidestep the man mastering him. Drake held the reins with a firm hand as he spoke gently to the animal, in a low tone that soothed but conveyed absolute command. Granting him grudging admiration as chills overcame her from the sound of his voice, tenderly guiding as she had once heard it, Ronnie led her bay out of the stable yard. Drake followed her with Black Satan under perfect control.

"The island covers about two miles," Ronnie said informatively. "We can ride up through the cliffs, or take the beach route. Either is a nice ride—"

"Ronnie."

Twisting her head quizzically at his halting, low tone, she arched a brow in question.

"I want to apologize." His eyes were as darkly fathomless as ever.

"For what?" she demanded shortly.

"For several of the things I said. I can't pretend I'm happy about this situation, or that I could ever condone your behavior, but I know there's more here than meets the eye. I have no right to judge you."

Ronnie kept her eyes glued to the trail in silence. What could she say? But he wanted a response. She heard an impatient oath from him, and then Black Satan trotted up alongside her. The house was far behind them now, hidden from their view by the dense foliage of the rising cliff. Drake passed her, reaching near Scheherazade's muzzle to catch her reins and stop the horse.

"Ronnie!" Drake persisted. "If you would talk to me, I might be able to do something."

"There is nothing that anyone can do," Ronnie said flatly, sighing as the horses strained at their bits. She raised her eyes imperiously. "I thank you for being so quick to assure Pieter. . . ." Then anger suddenly overtook her cool resolve. "What in the hell possessed you to sculpt—to sculpt—"

"More than met the eye?" Drake provided laconically. "I didn't do it on purpose, I promise you. I just knew, and my hands—"

"You sound like Pieter," Ronnie said with unintentional bitterness. "The hands of the artist just move."

Drake shrugged. "Something like that." His voice went hard and grim. "But I told you once I would never intentionally cause Pieter any pain. Whether you want to admit it to me or not, the man is dying. That is why I find it so terribly difficult to understand you."

"I don't remember asking you to understand me," Ronnie replied smoothly.

"No," Drake responded critically, adding in curt reminder, "but you are asking other things of me."

"Could you let go of my horse's reins, please?" Ronnie asked, preferring to ignore his statement. "I think we should take the beach path."

He had barely released his grip before she hugged her knees tightly to Scheherazade's ribs. The animal, attuned to her mistress's lightest touch, broke immediately into a smooth canter.

The black stallion was not far behind.

"Ronnie!"

Ignoring Drake's demanding shout, Ronnie continued on. She had no intention of enduring a question-and-answer period.

There was little else she could say to Drake; no way to redeem herself in his eyes.

The wind drove against her face, giving her a wonderful sensation of wild, abandoned freedom. Scheherazade moved beneath her with powerful magic. It was possible to believe she could race forever, away from the turmoil of her life, away from the man who now relentlessly pursued her.

"Ronnie!" he shouted again imperiously.

She glanced behind her quickly to see him scowling darkly. He was still shouting, but she couldn't make out the words. She didn't want to hear them anyway. The pounding of Scheherazade's sure hooves was tempestuous music to her ears. Breaking out of the trail through the foliage and onto the beach, she gave her horse full rein. Scheherazade, as exuberant for freedom as she, tore gladly into a thundering gallop.

Drake was still shouting. The mare was a powerful animal, but no match for the stallion. Ronnie was forced from her world of wind and speed to glance at Drake as Black Satan pounded abreast of the mare.

"Damn it, Ronnie—,"

She turned back around. Racing along the beach, she thought with irritation, and he was still determined to give her the third degree!

Impossible. He was still talking, but she couldn't make out the words. Scheherazade could hold her own. Ronnie was not going to give in to Drake; she would run until both she and the bay had tired, and Drake could go hang.

Racing was one of her great pleasures. Either on Scheherazade, or in the Boston Whaler, she loved the feel of wind and sea in her face. Riding on the beach was almost like combining the two. She could feel and hear the wonderful, vibrant gallop of the horse; she could feel and hear the infinite rolling of the surf; salt spray sailed into her face, and sand flew behind her. . . .

And Drake was still shouting for her to stop. He was telling her something, but she had closed off. Purposely.

The great black stallion pulled alongside of her again. "*Ronnie!*"

Still she ignored him. It was a contest of wills. It was one that she could win—they were on her turf.

He was furious, and she knew it. She loved it. She had enough of Pieter maneuvering her to his will, she'd be damned if she would find Drake anything more than mere annoyance.

She glanced to her right to give him a grim smile, but perplexity furrowed her brow instead. Something in his tone began to crack through the wall of of sound with which she had cocooned herself. "The gir—"

She lost the rest of his word, but she then noticed more than anger in his dark scowl. His bronze skin was stretched taut over his features, his brows seemed to meet in a single tight arch, and his lips were thin and white beneath the black curl of his mustache. He was concerned, frightened. . . .

Black Satan began to head her off into deeper water, forcing her to slow down just as a movement beneath her seat made her sickly aware of the word Drake had been saying. The girth was slipping on her saddle. In another few minutes she would be thrown under Scheherazade.

Drake reached for her reins just as she began to pull them in herself. The cinch belt gave entirely, and the polished leather saddle swerved awkwardly off the horse, dumping Ronnie unceremoniously into three feet of saltwater.

Sputtering, she thrashed around to regain her balance, and then stood, shivering despite the late summer heat. She was mortified—her appearance totally undignified—but embarrassment was far preferable to the broken bones that could have resulted had Drake not forced her to slow down in the deeper water. . . .

He leaped off his own horse, mindless of the water that filled his Frye boots and saturated his jeans, and strode toward her, grasping her in his arms as he reached her.

"I'm all right," she protested feebly as he lifted her off her feet and carried her to the white sand. "I'm all right," she repeated, gasping. But she didn't fight him. Her arms curled around his neck, she closed her eyes, unable to deny the pleasure of the stolen moment of being held by him, of feeling the pounding of his heart, of resting her head against the breadth of his chest and having his heat radiate new warmth through her.

All too soon she was lying on the beach. She lay still as his eyes raked over her, with tender caring. . . .

Briefly. Very briefly. A second later he was standing, legs apart and firmly planted in the sand, tight-knuckled hands clenched on his waist.

"Good Lord, woman! What the hell is the matter with you! Why didn't you listen to me? Of all the unmitigated fool things to do . . ." He railed on in the same tone, and Ronnie felt the chills—and any sense of grateful tenderness—drain from her swiftly as her own temper rose to match the dark, burning fury in his eyes. She took enough harassment from Pieter! And she took that for a reason! She'd be damned if she'd tolerate another man venting anger in her direction—deserved or not.

Springing to her feet and spraying Drake with water and sand with the the fury of her pounce, she marched straight to him, her own legs spread in a defiant stance, her arms flying with wild vehemence.

"Don't you dare—don't you dare!—speak to me like that! I won't have it. I will not have it! All right, so I should have listened, but how the hell did I know you had something to say that wasn't an insult or a none-of-your-business question? I have had it up to my neck, Mr. Drake O'Hara. You're right—you don't know a damn thing and you have no right on earth to judge me." Ronnie wasn't winding down at all. All the frustration and wrath she had so carefully bottled up rose to the surface and, before she knew it, she was pummeling Drake's chest with tight-ly clenched fists.

At first Drake was stunned. Then, absurdly, he broke into laughter, and continued to chuckle as he dodged her flailing fists and secured them easily with his own hands.

Then, as she ranted and raved and protested, newly infuriated by his amusement, he picked her up once more, carried her several feet in to the water, and dumped her back in, watching with that dry, sardonic smile as she sputtered again to the surface, gasping and incoherent as she slung a widespread string of oaths in to his face.

"Hey! Cool down," Drake protested, backing away from her with mock terror in his eyes. "I thought one dunking might do it, but another may be necessary."

"You dunk me one more time, Drake O'Hara," Ronnie dared, her eyes flashing with the brilliance of cut sapphires, "and I swear to God, you'll live to regret this day if it takes my entire lifetime!"

Her threat elicited nothing but more laughter, and she attempted to stomp a foot in the water before realizing how ridiculous she must look. Her cap was long gone with the waves, her hair was half up and half down with straggling pins, and her elegant fawn-colored riding habit encased her in drenched dishevelment.

Snapping her mouth shut for an instant, she drew herself to her full height and primly stiffened her shoulders. "Pray, Mr. O'Hara, be so kind as to tell me what you find so amusing about all this?"

He crossed his arms over his chest and slowly let eyes that still glittered with laughter roam with ill-concealed mirth from her hair-plastered face to the spot where her breeches met the water. "Besides the obvious?" he inquired innocently.

Gritting her teeth, Ronnie retorted, "Yes—besides the obvious!"

"Okay, my dear, dear Mrs. von Hurst," he replied, his mockery light as he surveyed her. "It's rather an inside joke, but I'll try to explain." He shifted his weight to launch into his explanation, and as Ronnie glared at him she was forced to hide a grudging admiration behind the wall of her anger. Even soaked he was magnificent, his form outlined by his wet clothing, his hair and mustache so black, they glinted blue.

"You see, I've always thought of you as a cat. So sleek, so

84

smooth, so independent . . . incredibly lithe, remarkably agile. From the moment I first saw you, I thought you possessed that sophisticated feline mystique. By whimsy I think I've just discovered that to be a little true." He paused for a moment, and Ronnie realized that he had been slowly advancing on her. His words had astounded her. They seemed to be compliments.

But that devilish twinkle was in his eyes. She began to back off further in to the water as he continued his approach.

"A cat, Ronnie," he continued. "An aloof creature, seeking to be stroked occasionally, only at her own leisure. Sometimes even purring with pleasure. Sometimes baring claws that scratch deeply, but always, always, so terribly independent."

He had woven a spell with his words as he came closer and closer. And even as she watched him with suspicion, he stopped directly in front of her and grinned, his teeth startlingly white against the damp mustache.

"Now I'm absolutely convinced you are a cat. Only a drowned cat could look so pathetic when inadvertently drenched."

Ronnie curled her lips over tightly clenched teeth, and her eyes blazed, shimmering like the sea beneath the sun. "Thank you, Drake," she enunciated with dry formality. "A cat, huh? I would watch it, then," she advised. "I've heard that cats are known to be exceptionally fierce when 'inadvertently drenched.' "

"Are they?"

"Oh, yes," she said pleasantly, basically back in control and wise enough to move with caution. "Especially when plagued by extremely dense, prying blackbirds." She certainly wasn't going to be able to use brute force against him, she decided dryly, but perhaps a little cat cunning. . . .

"Prying blackbirds," he told her with an edge to his voice, "only pry when they don't understand. It's an effort not to be dense."

She wasn't really listening, she was hiding a smile of satisfaction—he expected no retaliation. Shrugging dismissively, she stooped in the water as if to find a pebble in her boot, then leaned her weight abruptly against him as she shifted a foot behind his.

The effect was marvelous. Totally unprepared, Drake fell backward with a splash. Her self-satisfied smile of victory, however, left her face and was replaced with a yelp. He had recovered enough to catch her hand before he went down, and a split second later she was splashing down on top of him.

"Blackbirds can also be fierce when harassed by cats," Drake said, grinning as he maintained a grip upon her as they both surfaced. "Poor things. Especially when they fall prey to the deviousness of a cat. A second time." The grin suddenly left his lips. "Most especially cats who promise love in the dark, and forever in the daylight, while knowing all along that their promise of forever is nothing but a lark."

He still held her wrist; she couldn't escape him. The color fled from her face, and she lowered her lashes, but she didn't flinch.

"A part of me meant that, Drake," she admitted with a strange type of dignified pride. "I—I just never imagined—"

"That I'd appear at your house?" he demanded sarcastically, his grip upon her wrist tensing painfully.

"No." She straightened her shoulders and met his eyes. "I never imagined that you could possibly be serious."

Drake stared at her silently for several seconds, then cast her hand away from his with a strangled curse. God, he told himself with contempt, he was falling for her again, for her words that meant nothing.

"Oh?" he charged, knowing his anger rose even as he attempted to stay as cool as she was. "You're not going to ask my forgiveness—tell me you just went a little crazy? You had been contemplating leaving your cruel husband?"

"No." Ronnie didn't move. He had jokingly told her—before the conversation had turned grave—that she looked like a drowned cat. But she didn't. Pale, more regal than ever with her pride wrapped around her with her admissions, she still looked like marble, perfect, intricately sculpted marble. He was still in love with her, he still wanted her so desperately. Contempt was his only defense. He wanted to believe that she loved him, no matter how wrong.

"I have never once contemplated leaving Pieter," she said tonelessly.

There was misery to her voice, but truth; something so honest that he wanted to pull her comfortingly into his arms. But pain fed the fuel of his anger, the inner reminder that she had used him.

"Ahhh . . ." he murmured cruelly. "A greedy cat."

Ronnie felt as if she had been struck. Her entire body seemed to shudder uncontrollably. But she couldn't let Drake move in too closely—she had already offered what she could, an offering he disdained. "Have it your way, Drake," she said, shrugging.

He turned his back on her in the water, staring across the cliffs of the island. They must look like two idiots, he decided remotely, standing in waist-high surf, talking circles around each other. He had apologized for his treatment of her when they started out, and now he was back to it. It was sheer frustration that drove him, and he knew it. He hated home wreckers; he liked, respected, and admired Von Hurst.

If the man was a macho idiot who beat his wife, Drake could like himself better. But Von Hurst wasn't an idiot, nor was he insanely cruel. He loved his wife. The relationship wasn't right, but whatever the depths of emotion, Ronnie also cared for Von Hurst. Whether that caring was tempered by a vicarious hold on wealth and position, Drake just couldn't tell. . . .

Yet it was hard to question her beautiful, steadfast eyes; hard to convince himself she didn't love him, too. . . . For a moment he clenched his fists painfully at his side. With effort he released them. He turned back to find her motionless, watching him, still pale, still determinedly dignified.

"Sorry," he said simply, mentally giving him himself a shake. He would get to the bottom of everything, and he would live by his apology. She visibly relaxed at his abrupt change, and more than ever, he wanted just to touch her. "Oh, no!" he cried, quelling a grin.

87

"What?" she demanded quickly, concerned.

"My drowned cat is drying off!"

With the supple strength of a born athlete, he was swiftly upon her, lifting her in his arms a last time to dunk her thoroughly. She clasped her fingers over his head and dragged him down, too. They both emerged sputtering and laughing, their arms wound around one another as their eyes met. Such a contradiction! Ronnie thought, anger sparking in her. "Now, what do you find so vastly amusing?" she demanded haughtily, warily thinking of his lightning change of mood.

He sobered in an instant and his voice was strange when he answered. "You almost had me convinced that you were marble," he told her quietly. "I had begun to believe that I had imagined there had been a woman who walked, talked, and breathed with beautiful life and warmth. . . ."

He withdrew his arms tiredly and strode out of the water, whistling for the horses as he reached the shore. Ronnie stared after him, chewing her bottom lip. His shirt and jeans were plastered to his body, and it was impossible not to feel a tug at her heart and senses as she observed the striking tone and pride of his physique. But it would also be impossible ever to explain all that she felt. Still, all anger seeped from her, and she determined to grasp whatever straw of friendship that she could from him.

Ronnie began to chuckle, emerging from the water as Drake captured the bay, restored its saddle, and then went after the stubborn stallion.

Drake scowled at her as he made a second attempt to catch Black Satan's trailing reins. "You want to let me in on *your* amusement?" he inquired wryly.

Inclining her head toward the horse, Ronnie smiled. "Just the obvious."

Drake didn't look at her, but his own smile slipped slowly back to curve his lips. He moved one hand to gently pat the stallion's neck while the other snaked out to secure the reins. "Need a boost up?" he asked Ronnie.

She thought about saying yes just for an excuse to feel his touch, but she shook her head. "No, thanks. I can manage."

They began the ride back to the house in a silence that was strangely comfortable. Nearing the stable yard, Ronnie stopped him.

"Drake."

"Yes?" He turned to her expectantly.

"I—it's my turn to apologize. I could have been really hurt. Thank you."

He gave her a cocky, devilish grin that mocked his own emotion. "'Twas nothing, my marble beauty. A pleasure."

Their eyes met for an instant and then they both looked away.

Neither had anything more to say. They had reached the stable, and the strange, compelling interlude was over.

CHAPTER FIVE

Pieter did not appear for dinner that night, only his note of apology upon a filigreed silver tray. And, of course, the note was addressed to Drake, not Ronnie.

She watched as Drake's dark eyes scanned Pieter's flourished script quickly as they waited in the salon, and she did not avert her gaze when his eyes rose from the paper to her.

"It seems," he said laconically, absently folding the sheet of monogrammed note paper, "that your husband wishes a few days of rest. It's his suggestion that we spend the day in Charleston tomorrow."

Ronnie's fingers curled over the arm of her chair. She was sure Pieter was not issuing a suggestion but a command.

"Surely you've seen Charleston," she murmured.

He shrugged, tapping the note against a casually crossed knee. "Not much of it, really. I came here to see Pieter. I was a few days ahead of schedule, so . . ."

His sentence trailed away, but Ronnie knew the ending. Flushing unhappily, she lowered her eyes to the upholstery of her chair, where she watched a long glazed nail trace the pattern of the brocade material.

"I think we should go into Charleston," Drake said with a firm determination that made Ronnie's heart leap unexpectedly. His tone held an underlying menace. She was sure she was in for the third degree again, which Drake wouldn't administer in the house with the possibility of others listening in.

Stiffening, she answered indifferently. "If you wish." She resented him heartily. He must realize that if she protested, Pieter might become suspicious. Why the hell couldn't he do the gentlemanly thing and disappear into the blue—or at least think of sound reasons to reject his host's "suggestions" when he threw the two of them together?

"Yes"—he looked her squarely in the eye—"I do wish."

Henri appeared to announce dinner, and Drake rose mockingly, offering her his arm. Ronnie clenched her teeth as they entered the dining room together and sat down to their lone meal. Drake's conversation became impersonal and polite—the front he extended for Henri and Gretel as they entered and exited the room.

Ronnie knew his smooth mask would not slip, but she ate and spoke in stilted misery anyway. Each time she glanced his way she caught his dark eyes upon her, pensive and calculating. And she shivered with new apprehension of the morning to come.

Dave Quimby took them into Charleston Harbor on the boat at ten o'clock. Pieter kept a Ferrari parked in a private lot, and Ronnie suggested they pick up the car and head first for the old slave market.

Drake firmly shook his head. "I think we should start with a walk along the Battery. I want to talk to you."

Ronnie sighed with sheer exasperation, her gaze upon the shimmering harbor and the multitude of boats rocking lightly in their berths.

"Drake, you can talk to me until you're blue in the face! There is nothing that I can tell you."

"There's plenty that you can tell me," he insisted grimly, taking her elbow and starting briskly down the walk by the sea. "And I definitely intend to get some answers."

Powerless against his hold, Ronnie had no choice but to accompany him.

"For a man who proclaimed he'd never touch me with a ten-foot pole," Ronnie complained with bitter sarcasm, "you're doing quite a job on my arm." Though long-limbed herself, she was panting to keep up with his brisk pace.

"Merely expression," he replied laconically. "I think we both know to what type of touching I was referring." He halted abruptly. "This looks as good a place as any." Bowing sardonically, he dusted sand from the seawall. "Sit, if you will, please, Mrs. von Hurst." At her hesitance he raised a mocking brow. "Or might we crease our designer jeans?"

Ronnie glared at him coldly, then pointedly drew her eyes to the label of his black jeans before returning her eyes to his and caustically replying, "I don't know, might we?"

The darkness of his eyes suffused with a flame of mirth as his mustache twitched in a way she was beginning to know very well. "My dear Mrs. von Hurst," he replied gallantly, "I do give you credit for a marvelously ticking little mind." He crouched to the wall, deftly flinging his legs over the edge while dragging her down beside him. He didn't release her hand as she joined him with little choice, her attitude less than gracious, her teeth grinding.

He smiled at her annoyance. "This is a lovely view," he commented, his mustache tilting with a full grin. "The sea, the sky, the mist, Fort Sumter rising in the distance. Nice place for a talk."

Ronnie kept her gaze on Fort Sumter, rising in the mist as he had pointed out. "Lovely," she agreed dryly. "Talk any time you like."

"How long has Pieter been ill?"

Ronnie shrugged, determined to give him nothing. "Awhile."

Drake muttered something inaudible beneath his breath and his grip on her hand jerked painfully. "Damn it, Ronnie! I already know the man is desperately ill. I'm not asking you for the sake of conversation—I think I can help."

The explosive sincerity of his voice was undeniable. Ronnie glanced at him, reading the intensity of his dark stare, then shook her head with appreciative but sad resignation. "Drake,

I told you before. There's nothing that you can do, nothing that *anyone* can do."

"Ronnie," Drake said forcefully, "you're being fatalistic. I can help. I know a man from the center at Johns Hopkins who specializes in just this type of thing, the wasting diseases—sclerosis."

"But Pieter has seen dozens of doctors!"

"So he should see a dozen more."

Ronnie mulled his words slowly through her mind. Drake was right; she and Pieter had given up, accepted the inevitable. They should have never allowed themselves to do so. Such a fight should be fought to the bitter end. "How do we get Pieter to see this man, and will he see Pieter?"

"The doctor will see Pieter," Drake said assuredly, softening his features to a grin again. "He's an art lover. Pieter—well, leave him to me."

"No!" Ronnie cried. "He'll know I've been discussing him and he'll be absolutely livid."

Drake shook his head emphatically, and Ronnie suddenly realized he was no longer gripping her hand but holding it soothingly, his fingers working tenderly over the pale lines of her veins. "I promise you, Pieter will know nothing. . . ." His voice trailed away as they both thought of the other implication of such a statement.

Drake cleared his throat and continued in a businesslike tone. "I'll talk to Pieter and convince him of what is really the truth— I can see his condition. But what I do need from you is everything that you can tell me. I want to know when he became ill, how the illness affects him, and what has been said so far by his doctors."

"That's a large order," Ronnie murmured. "Where do I begin?" She wanted to help Drake, knowing he was serious and reaching tentatively for the ray of hope he was giving her. And she would answer him as truthfully as possible, but there were certain things she simply couldn't reveal, certain things

93

about which Pieter would rather die than have become known. . . .

"Start anywhere," Drake prompted her, "and I'll insert questions when I want you to go further."

Taking a deep breath, Ronnie began to talk, telling him that the disease had begun at a slow rate of acceleration soon after their marriage. It was a small white lie, one which she hoped would make no difference. Drake's few comments and questions were intelligent and well spaced, and before she knew it, she became immersed in her monologue, telling Drake the things that worried her most, confiding in him as she had never thought possible.

They never had to discuss a sex life at all. Drake knew Pieter and Ronnie kept separate quarters, and although Ronnie knew Drake still condemned her for her affair with him aboard the ship, he was tactful enough at the moment to make no remarks.

Ronnie stopped speaking suddenly and looked up into his eyes, which gazed intently at her. She wondered if she caught a spark of empathy, but it was gone so quickly, she assured herself that tenderness from him could only exist in her imagination. And yet, she felt good, as if talking had lifted a heavy load from her shoulders. She could easily hate Drake for his often disdainful treatment of her, but she also trusted him explicitly.

He was a hard man, a thorough man—a man she had stupidly fallen in love with—a man of fury and intensity, but one who would direct his energies tirelessly and relentlessly in pursuit of a goal. She felt a drained relief to know his goal at that moment was the life and health of Pieter von Hurst.

"It hasn't been easy for you, has it?" he asked, his tone surprisingly hard for his question.

"No, it hasn't," Ronnie replied bluntly, her voice every bit as matter-of-fact. Then the relief of having shared her burden washed through her and she impetuously grabbed his arm and stared into his dark eyes beseechingly. "Oh, Drake, do you really think there's any kind of a chance? . . ."

"Yes, Ronnie, I do. I believe there is always hope."

Hope. Ronnie dropped his arm and stared out to sea. For some things, perhaps, there was hope. Not for others.

Drake suddenly hopped to his feet with athletic agility and reached to give her a hand. "I've never seen Fort Sumter," he told her, still with a rather harsh, gravelly tone. "Can we go over? How do we get there?"

Ronnie stood beside him and answered his new line of questioning levelly, sounding something like an indifferent tour guide in relation to his manner. No matter what he said, no matter what had once gone on between them—no, not even the fact that they had become conspirators on Pieter's behalf—could change his opinion of her. For a wild moment of misery she was tempted to throw herself into his arms and explain everything, to unburden herself completely, to cry out that she wasn't a run-a-round wanton but a victim herself of desperate need . . . and love. But she could say none of those things. She simply couldn't do it to Pieter and, anyway, it wouldn't change things, she would still be Mrs. Pieter von Hurst.

Even with the slim ray of hope Drake offered, Ronnie would always be bound to Pieter by ties of her own morality. And so as her mind dwelt upon dreams unuttered she kept up a line of chatter about Charleston, talking as she led him to the Ferrari, which would be their transportation around town. She pointed out various old houses along the Battery as they drove to the ferry that would take them out to Fort Sumter, maintaining her cool, instructorlike stream of exposition.

As Drake listened to her, he struggled with an inward battle. He didn't mean to sound harsh each time he spoke; his cold brusqueness was a line of defense. It was impossible to look into the incredible blue depths of her eyes and not be touched—and painfully inflamed. He decided with a cruel twist of his lips that he was a masochist.

Every time he came near her, he was stricken with the wild desire to sweep her into his arms and take her with primitive passion—no matter where they happened to be. Remembrance of the satin softness of her skin, the perfect, harmonious fit her slender, lusciously curved form made with his body . . . being one with her . . . drove him to the brink of madness, and to a number of cold showers. And all the while he berated himself for his stupidity. She was Von Hurst's wife; a sophisticated woman who indulged in affairs for her own entertainment while married to the great, ailing artist. . . .

God, he groaned inwardly. Why the hell didn't she fit the part of the hard, calculating seductress? It would be so easy to forget her then . . . but no one could look into her unmasked, depthless, beguiling eyes and call her hard, or believe that she was—what she was.

A woman with needs, a part of his mind told him. One who endured a lonely, demanding life. One who sincerely cared for Pieter. But he had been deceived by her once, used by her once, because he had trusted the character and soul in those eyes, which had held him a willing prisoner of her grace and beauty.

He couldn't lower his guard to her for a second. She was Von Hurst's. But deep within himself he struggled with another thought. If—an incredible if—he could ever make her his, she would probably do the same—run around. She had learned the lesson, and surely cheating could only become easier and easier. He didn't even have any idea of how many escapades she had carried on like the one they had shared.

He shook himself mentally. She wasn't his. He had no right to be angry with her; her affairs or lack of them were Pieter's concern. Her *husband's* concern. He lashed out at her because of his own frustration and a haunting desire that overwhelmed him that could never be fulfilled again. . . .

Recognizing what ripped him apart—and admitting the root of his anger—suddenly calmed him. She was here with him today because he had forced her hand, both to quiz her on Pieter, and also to take a form of punishment out on her—to force her to be near him. Perhaps he wanted to force her to suffer as he did, because he loved her still every bit as much as he hated her for shattering the illusion of trust and happiness he had created with her upon his pedestal. . . .

"Drake."

He started as she said his name, obviously for a second time. "This is it," she said quietly as he stared at her blankly in return. "The ferry."

"Oh." Drake uncoiled his length and hastened dexterously from the car, suddenly determined to be courteous. But she was out of the driver's seat before he could reach her door. Not daunted, he slipped an arm through hers. The glance she gave him, peering at an angle through fringed lashes, was skeptical, to say the least.

"I'm opting for a pleasant day," he told her smoothly. "A tourist out with a native to see the sights. No past, no concerns. Deal?"

Ronnie slightly arched a doubting brow and pursed her lips in a small smirk, but nodded. "No past, no concerns."

And an hour later, as they crawled around the cannons and ruined brick of the island fort, she lost her cynicism and began to believe him. He was out to be charming.

They linked arms as they ambled about, occasionally listening to the guides, occasionally referring to the informative pamphlets, and reading aloud to one another. They discussed the war and the battle that had rocked Fort Sumter over a century ago, and from there the conversation progressed easily to present times. Without innuendo, Drake quizzed Ronnie on life in Paris, and she in turn discovered that he was well traveled and had a host of amusing anecdotes relating to difficulties for Americans in various European cities.

By the time the ferry took them back to the harbor, they were both comfortable with their strange truce. Drake assuredly plucked the keys from Ronnie's hand as they returned to the Ferrari, murmuring with a quiet firmness, "I'll drive."

"Oh?" she teased, obediently slipping into the passenger seat as he opened her door, "and where are we going?"

"I do know the town a little bit," he retorted. "And I know precisely where to go for dinner, dressed as we are."

Ronnie glanced ruefully at the jeans they both wore. She

hadn't thought that they would be dining out, but they had passed lunchtime without thought, and she realized she was ravenous. She was also happy to continue the day. It had had a shaky start, but the afternoon had been so pleasant; a sweet interlude of a dream coming unexpectedly to life. In time they would return to the island, her coach would turn back into a pumpkin, her prince would turn back into Drake, and she would turn back into Mrs. Pieter von Hurst.

But the bewitching time was midnight, wasn't it? she thought, closing her eyes dreamily. Drake was taking her to dinner. It was a pity they weren't dressed. She would love to dance every second away and, like Cinderella, not lose a precious second, but leave on the stroke of twelve. . . .

"Where are we going?" she asked, her lips slightly curled from the whimsy of her imaginings. "There aren't any really nice dinner spots I know of where we can go like this."

Drake sent her a dancing ebony glance. "It takes a tourist!" he groaned with mock disgust. "We are going to a little private club near the city center. A casual place with impeccable stuffed mushrooms and the tenderest steak tidbits you'll ever sink your teeth into. And"—his sizzling coal gaze came her way again as if he had read her mind—"they employ a top forties band that is great. They lean a little toward hard rock, but they are good, and lots of fun. Any objections?"

Ronnie shook her head and lowered her lashes to hide the extreme pleasure his words had given her. "No—no objections. It does sound like fun."

The club really wasn't little at all, Ronnie realized as they entered the comfortable redwood establishment. Like so many night spots, the decor was dark, basically black and crimson, and the lighting dim. It was split into several sections, with the band and dance floor a half level below the dinner tables. Ronnie approved of the design immediately. It was possible to talk with one's partner while intimately dining without being drowned out by the music, and then equally possible to fully enjoy the dancing and music without intruding on a voracious diner!

They were led up a short flight of thickly carpeted stairs to a secluded booth in a corner. The smiling hostess seated them across from one another, and Ronnie was grateful as she sank into the plush booth. It would be too easy to forget she was just a Cinderella if she had to sit next to him and feel the heat from his body vibrate along the side of hers. And she was sure Drake never really forgot who she was, no matter how pleasantly he behaved toward her.

A silence fell between them after they placed their drink orders, and Ronnie pretended a great interest in her menu while sneaking covert glances at Drake. He was marvelous—though somewhat chilling—just to look at. Tonight he almost matched the decor of the club; his snug jeans were black, his casually tailored shirt black-and-red-patterned. The top two buttons of his shirt were open, revealing a V of crisp black hair upon his chest. Matching it all were his eyes, seeming of the deepest, darkest, ebony fire. With his wavy dark-brown hair and devilishly curved mustache, high, gaunt cheeks and foreboding but fascinating profile, he had already drawn the recurring gazes of the club's female patrons.

Yet it was more than looks that brought eyes to him like magnets. A sense of indifferent confidence was part of Drake. He emanated a totally male assurance, and something even more intriguing: that beguiling, mesmerizing look of the devil—a dangerous look, as compelling as fire. . . .

A hand, long and broad and sporting neatly clipped nails, suddenly swept away Ronnie's red-tassled menu. "You're reading upside down," Drake told her dryly, adding as she flushed and parted her lips for an explanation, "And you don't need to read anyway. Trust me, I won't lead you astray."

Glad of any excuse to bypass his observation of her upside-down reading habits, Ronnie inanely murmured, "I trust you." Then, alarmed at the multiple meanings her tone could give to the simple words, she chatted on at an impetuous rate. "Stuffed mushrooms, right? And the most tender steak tidbits in the world. Served, I assume, with some type of deliciously seasoned dipping sauce. And the mushrooms—stuffed with fresh crab-meat, delicately tipped with bread crumbs, and basted in sea-soned butter to tempt, tease, and fully arouse the palate—" She broke off in confusion, wondering where she had found such words of description for food.

Drake was laughing. "They should hire you to write the menus. You just made a casual dinner sound like an erotic experience."

His laughter broke off abruptly, and it was he who stared down at his menu. They could both easily remember an erotic experience. Thankfully their drinks arrived at the table before an uncomfortable silence could lengthen. Drake glanced at Ronnie only once as he gave their orders. He already knew she preferred her meat rare, sour cream for her baked potato.

Ronnie staunchly pulled her flustered demeanor together as Drake placed the order for their meal. A long sip of the brandy alexander she now had before her helped her regain a measure of aloofness, necessary with their words taking on unintentional insinuation. She didn't want to mar the day with a tense ex-change of hostilities should one of them step too far.

The sweet, mellow taste of her drink hid but didn't diminish the combined potency of the brandy and crème de cacao, which were mixed with only a hint of cream. A second sip steadied her while giving her the illusion of relaxation as a languorousness misted the world around her, taking away all the sharp edges. She almost giggled but stopped herself. She was floating on two sips of a drink, and she could only credit the sensation to her completely empty stomach.

She didn't want to giggle right now, though; she wanted to wear her cool image, her Mrs. Pieter von Hurst image. A giggle just wouldn't fit. Nor would the rumble in her stomach if it became loud enough to be heard. . . .

Placing an elbow on the table and resting her chin on her knuckles, Ronnie smiled distantly, unaware that the sparkling, wistful mist in her eyes was soft and bewitching. "Tell me," she said conversationally, "something about Drake O'Hara." She idly picked up the swizzle stick that had been in her drink and pushed absently at the floating nutmeg. Ruefully, her eyes then on the drink, she added, "You know a little too much about me, and I know nothing about you. Except that your home is Chicago."

He quirked a brow as she met his eyes again. "Not fair. I don't really know anything about you. Not about the real Ronnie who hides behind the marble mask. I know nothing about your past, about your own dreams."

Ronnie bit down lightly on her lower lip in an imperceptible movement of an eyetooth. It was a damn good thing he knew nothing about her dreams. They were as far fetched as a piece of the moon.

"You first," she told him. "Were you born in Chicago?"

"Right in the heart," he replied wryly, lounging back in the booth, one finger running idly up and down the icy moisture on the side of his rock glass. "I grew up in a suburb, Des Plaines, and then picked up my B.A. at Northwestern." He grimaced ruefully. "My major was actually business, but I was offered an art scholarship to the University of Florence. I picked up a master's degree there and became passionately involved in what I had previously decided—wisely, as my parents had instructed —to be only a hobby: sculpture. It was impossible not to become aggressively and passionately involved, not with the works of Michelangelo and other great Italian masters within reaching distance. I used to spend hours in the Medici Chapels, just staring at his work on the tombs."

"I don't understand," Ronnie interjected. "You must be very good. Pieter says so, and he never flatters anyone, and you received a scholarship. Why do you only dabble in sculpture now?"

Drake shrugged. "Actually, I don't just dabble. I work under another name. Mero."

Ronnie had lifted her glass to sip at her drink and found herself taking a huge swallow—one that left her choking as the heat of the brandy catapulted to her stomach. "Mero!" she gasped. He *was* well known in the world of sculpture, and highly respected. Pieter had many of his pieces, fine miniatures intricately wrought in flawless marble. "I had no idea . . ."

"Few people do," Drake said. "I prefer to remain anonymous. As a gallery owner and critic, it becomes awkward to be known. I would appreciate your keeping my alter ego a confidence."

"Certainly," Ronnie murmured, surprised and inordinately pleased that he should trust her enough to offer such a confidence. If only he could trust her a little as far as other things went. . . . Foolish. What good would it do? She couldn't change her own circumstances. She blocked her mind to pain and asked, "But then, why the galleries?"

He laughed. "I'm a little too self-centered to be a completely dedicated artist. My love of art is widespread. I'm fascinated by the work of others, by the ancient masters, by the promising greats of the future. When I can discover a talent, and force that talent to expand and improve, I receive my greatest personal rewards. And when I can work with or encourage a Pieter von Hurst, I find my own personal achievement."

"I don't find that self-centered at all," Ronnie murmured appreciatively, too enamored of his tale to make an attempt to sound indifferent. "I think it's wonderful."

Drake grinned. "Thanks. Your turn."

"My turn?" she echoed in dismay. "Not yet! You haven't really told me anything, uh . . ."

"Personal?"

"Well, yes, I suppose that is what I mean," she admitted. The drink, the cozy atmosphere, the muted sound of the band, all were making her unwittingly at ease with him, and bold enough to honestly pry. Her questions, she realized with a tug of pain, were part of a driving curiosity she couldn't contain, even as she accepted the fact weakly that the answers could cause agony. He said once, in another world, that he loved her. She didn't want to hear that he loved elsewhere, or that he had loved before, but with perverse voraciousness she had to know everything that she

102

could about him; about his life, about the things that made up the man that he was.

"Personal . . . hmm," he mused reflectively. "My parents are both living. They're a nice middle-class couple with a certain quiet charm who still reside in Des Plaines. I have two brothers and a sister, all younger, and the family meets each year for Christmas and the Fourth of July. You see, Katie lives in Arizona, Michael in Atlanta, and Padraic in northern Michigan. I have a lovely—if sometimes monstrous—collection of nieces and nephews."

Ronnie laughed at his monologue, envying him the obvious warmth of his family. Apparently Drake had everything: success of his own creation, wealth, power, and, most important, an abundance of love. The desolation of her own life threatened to sweep over her, so she quickly joked, "And are these lovely but monstrous little nieces and nephews all dark as Satan like their hell-bent uncle?"

Drake shrugged wide shoulders, flashing her a white grin at the comment. "Half and half. Perfect split. Padraic and I are dark like my father, Katie and Michael are blue-eyed blonds. Their offspring are all the various shades in between."

"Prolific family," Ronnie said dryly, sounding light in spite of the catch in her throat. "What happened to the oldest O'Hara? No little creations to date?"

"You would have known if there were," he told her bluntly, reminding her of the intimacy of their first meeting. Yes, he would have told her if he had any children. At that encounter, he had said that he wanted to marry her. . . .

"You could have been married at one time," she said defensively, playing with her swizzle stick again to avoid his eyes. "I mean, you are well over twenty-one, and a healthy, virile male . . ." Ronnie's voice trailed away and she was thoroughly annoyed to feel a hot flush rising to her cheeks again. She deserved this loss of cool reserve. She was asking leading questions that could only return in circular fashion to their own brief relationship, and consequently to the tension that lurked beneath their best efforts to be continually pleasant. For her to make a comment about his being a healthy, virile male was abject stupidity. She knew what he was, but he also knew that she knew only too well what he was. . . .

"No," he replied bluntly, "I have no children. I was married once, though, when I was very young."

Ronnie waited for him to continue, but he didn't, and she was compelled to ask in a soft whisper, "What happened?"

"She died," he said shortly, then catching the quickly hidden flicker of pain in Ronnie's eyes, he added, "My wife was an Italian girl. I met her while studying in Florence. There was a cholera outbreak."

"I'm sorry," Ronnie murmured truthfully, her eyes misting ridiculously.

"It was a long time ago," Drake said gruffly, watching her eyes as they shimmered with that soulful tragedy he had sensed before. Intuitively he knew she had suffered a similar loss, a pain that was not related to Pieter. He reached a forceful but strangely compassionate hand across the table to take hers. "Your turn, Ronnie. What happened to you before Pieter?"

She looked for a barb in his tone, or cynicism in his eyes, but there was neither. She shrugged and smiled softly. "The same. I lost a fiancé." Her lower lip trembled slightly.

"What happened?" He returned her own question.

She bit her trembling lower lip to cease its action. "Drugs," she said faintly. "I never even knew until it was too late and all the signs were there."

Drake's handclasp on hers shook roughly, and with surprise she found an unusual and oddly harsh sympathy in his eyes. "Surely you don't blame yourself!" he said sternly.

"No," she replied, startled at the realization that she did in a way. "Not really."

"Not at all," he commanded. "No one can change a situation like that."

Ronnie broke his gaze with a tentative smile of thanks, moving her eyes with sudden interest to the stage. Their conversation had grown a little too personal, and she didn't want her soul completely bared to this man who still condemned her on one hand while offering encouragement on the other.

"The band is marvelous," she offered enthusiastically. "And, if I'm not mistaken, we no longer have to starve. I believe our waitress is coming our way."

Her intent to change the subject was obvious, but as their dinner arrived, steaming with succulent aromas, her switch to a lighter, more casual conversation seemed easily accomplished. But after munching into and savoring a large mushroom cap, Drake returned to his interrogation of her with a single-worded question.

"Parents?"

"Pardon?" Ronnie stopped uneasily, her fork halfway to her mouth.

"Your parents. Are they living?"

She bit into her mushroom and shook her head. "They were killed in an auto crash in my senior year of high school."

Drake offered no more sympathy; it wasn't needed, he knew. Still, he felt his heart constricting for her and was consumed with an overwhelming desire to take her into his arms and shield her, protect her, and offer her all the love she had lost. He understood now the strength of her marble beauty, the brick wall of dignity that hid the giving, sensuous woman he had known so briefly.

But she wasn't his to protect or love. She was Pieter's. And she had never denied the love she felt for the husband she saw fit to leave from time to time.

"Siblings?" he asked, continuing to eat.

"None."

"What took you to Paris?"

"After college, I had nothing to go home to," she said matter-of-factly. "I majored in the French language, so it seemed logical to go to Paris. I met Jamie at The Louvre one day."

"And Pieter?"

"Through Jamie. He was a student." Ronnie set her fork down for a moment, losing her appetite for the delicious food. Like she had done, Drake was going to keep quizzing until he had all his answers. These were things she could answer honestly, so she might as well give him a quick story.

"Jamie and Pieter were close friends," she told Drake tonelessly, her hands folded in her lap, her eyes downcast. "When Jamie died, I was stunned, very young, and very lost. Pieter helped me through all the bad times. I'm—ah—I'm very grateful to him; I will never forget how wonderful he was."

"Von Hurst is an amazing man," Drake said simply.

Ronnie was still staring at her plate of half-eaten food, and so she didn't see the speculative look Drake covertly cast her way.

And he was speculating. For the first time since he had seen Ronnie beside his host, he had stopped envying Pieter von Hurst. Ronnie, he realized, did love the man. But not the way a man wanted to be loved. Her love for Von Hurst was gratitude, mingled with fondness and respect. It was not the all-encompassing passion and commitment that should exist, not the sharing, not two souls soaring . . . not the love, he, Drake, could have shared with her.

A savagery gripped Drake, an emotion he controlled by cruelly ripping at a piece of meat with his knife and fork. Ronnie had married Von Hurst, no matter what her emotions, for better or worse. But her vow hadn't held her when "worse" had come into being. All his speculations were absurd, they were to no end. . . . If she were suddenly as free as a lark, he wondered if he could ever learn to trust her.

He chewed his last piece of meat and pushed his plate aside, once more leaning back in the booth with crossed arms. "Enjoying the band?"

Ronnie glanced up to discover from his guarded ebony eyes that he had entirely withdrawn from her. "Yes, thank you," she replied coolly, "very much."

"Not too raucous for you?"

"No." She laughed. Drake had been right. The band, a five-member group consisting of a solid drummer, a keyboard player, two guitarists exchanging the vocal leads, and a talented saxophonist, tended to hard rock. They were careful to slip pleasant, mellow pieces into their repertoire, but they excelled at letting loose, playing popular pieces by The Stones, old Doors numbers, and other music that seemed tonight to stir wildly in her blood. Concentrating on the band, she forgot the air of aloofness that had settled over Drake and laughed. "I'm crazy about the band. They're making me feel very young."

Drake, caught by the vibrant yearning in her tone, laughed in return. "You can't be all that old!"

She tilted her head and quirked a shrugging brow. "I'll be thirty, and I know, that's not all that old. But they're making me feel really young—eighteen and, and . . ."

"Innocent again?" Drake supplied.

"Yes, I suppose that's what I mean."

Drake grinned with the satanish twinkle to his eyes. "Want to feel even younger? Let's try out the dance floor."

"Oh, I don't know," Ronnie demurred, watching the swirling dancers. "I'm not really sure what they're doing out there."

"Believe me"—Drake chuckled—"neither are they. These days, everyone does more or less what they feel like. Come on. Follow me, and I'll think of something."

He was on his feet, towering over her and reaching to escort her from her seat before she could protest further. His hand was on the small of her back as he led her down the short flight of steps and through the lower level to the shiny, light-colored wooden dance floor.

Just his touch was jolting. His hand upon her back sent traitorous tingles of anticipation and delighted memory racing along her spine. It was so natural to be touched by Drake, to drift into the warm masculinity of his arms, to curl her fingers at his nape.

The tune was a fast one, easily recognizable, and as he spun her about in deft circles, Drake laughingly informed her that the song had become popular after the movie *Saturday Night Fever*, and that it was a piece by the Bee Gees.

Panting as she dipped and swung and swirled, Ronnie haughtily replied, "I knew it was the Bee Gees! Even on the island we have a television—several actually—and a stereo system!"

"Did you see the movie?" Drake queried when another swoop of his arm brought them facing each other again.

"No!" she admitted, chuckling. She couldn't begin to imagine Pieter sitting through an American movie. "Did you?"

"Of course. Several times, actually." His grin broadened deeply. "I told you I had a score of nephews and nieces."

Ronnie laughed again, breathlessly. It was fun out here with Drake. It was almost as if—as if they were back on the boat; as if they had returned to that magical day when it had been her right to touch Drake, to feel Drake's touch upon her. . . .

The music rose to a pitch and clamored to a halt. "Slowin' down now," one vocalist called cheerfully. "One for all the lovers out there. . . ."

Before the young man had finished speaking, Ronnie felt herself crushed closely into Drake's arms, her entire form pressed to the warmth of his hard, strong body. Instinctively she arched to his hold upon her hips, nestling her head in the inviting curve of his shoulder. They danced silently, their movements synchronized, fluid with the tender beat of the music. Drake's hands moved caressingly along Ronnie's back, and with intuitive volition, her hands, once more resting around his neck, began an exploratory return. The silky sheerness of his shirt enhanced the play of hot muscles beneath her fingers, and she thrilled as she trailed them over his shoulders, then thread them through the thick hair at the back of his neck. She was dimly aware that she was being foolish, following a path that could lead nowhere. But she couldn't help herself. Her own arousal from the dance had to be apparent to Drake; her nipples, brushing against the heat and breadth of his chest, attuned to the crisp mat of curls that tickled them erotically despite the material of their clothing, were hardening to impertinent pebbles that seemed to reach out for further delectable contact. And she was quivering . . . burning with the heat his body lent to hers. . . .

She was too close to him not to feel the desire rising inside him.

108

But he said nothing; he made no movement to draw away. If anything, he pulled her irrevocably closer. His warm breath fanned against her hair, stirring new sensations of longing. Was it wistful thinking, or did his lips form a kiss at her temple? She had no way of knowing. Her eyes were closed, her face pressed against his shoulder, feeling heat, feeling the beautiful, lulling pounding of his heart—feeling, absorbing, becoming one with every breath he took. It was torture, it was agony, it was wonderful. She was secure and content, ablaze with an unquenchable fire. It didn't matter. She wanted the dance to go on and on. As long as the music played with the incessant beat of the drums, she was in an exotically haunting heaven.

She must have had mind control, a powerful telepathic bond with the band leader. The next three numbers, which finished the set, were slow, romantic tunes. They came to her ears infinitely sweetly. Never once did Drake break his hold. She was immersed in him, cocooned in his drugging body heat, intoxicated with the woodsy scent he wore that combined so well with his essence of virility.

Unknown to her, Drake's mind was running along the same lines. As long as the music played on, he could forget the world, and luxuriate in sheer sensation. Each time he inhaled, the air was sweet with the light perfume of her hair; each time he moved she molded to fit his body, her incredibly soft but firm curves taunting him with captivation. God, he wanted her. No other woman had affected him so totally, stirring his blood intensely at mere sight, reducing him to yearning with a simple touch or a look from shimmering eyes as depthless as the oceans. . . .

If he had to think, it would be wrong. But as long as the music played, he didn't have to think. He could hold her, feel the sensuous femininity of her straining breasts against his chest, the undulating fluidity of her hips against his. . . .

No, he didn't have to think. He couldn't possibly think. This little bit of ecstasy was his.

But the music did stop. He didn't meet her eyes, and she kept her head lowered as he swiveled her around and silently led her back to their booth, his hands still searing as they rested near the base of her spine. Without asking her consent, he ordered them each another drink.

He needed a drink. She must, too. Their contact was broken, and it was as if the sun had set on a cold day, leaving both empty and numb.

Drake glanced at his wristwatch with a frown. "We'd better drink up and head back. It's almost midnight." He opened his mouth and then shut it. He had been about to say "Your husband might be worried." But he couldn't phrase it that way. It would be a sacrilege at the moment. He started over. "I don't want Pieter to worry."

Ronnie smiled wryly in return, sighing silently with resignation. Midnight. Did everyone know that that was the bewitching hour? At the stroke of twelve, would all be lost?

Irrevocably. There was no glass slipper.

"Yes," she said smoothly, unconsciously straightening in the booth. Her chin tilted a little. "We'd better get going."

Drake payed the check and escorted her from the club. He took the wheel of the Ferrari without comment, so like Drake, always in charge.

They spoke little as they drove to the dock. Ronnie was exhausted. It was all she could do simply to stay awake. She didn't dare sleep; she was afraid she would convince herself that her dreams could be a reality and awaken to a devastating nightmare —reality.

Dave was sound asleep in the cabin of the Boston Whaler, but he cheerfully awoke as they came aboard, anxiously inquiring if they had had a nice day.

Even Dave liked Drake, Ronnie thought wearily.

Drake answered for them both, apologizing for being so late, assuring Dave they had had a wonderful day.

"No apologies necessary, Mr. O'Hara," Dave proclaimed with a proud grin. "Don't matter to me what part of the sea I'm on, so long as I can feel the water beneath me. As long as Miss

Veronica is happy and looked after, you stay anywhere as late as you like."

Drake voiced polite thanks and sat topside along with Ronnie. "Are you cold?" he inquired, his distant courtesy reinstated.

Ronnie shook her head. The night wind as they left the harbor was cold and brisk, but she welcomed its slapping chill and the salt spray it carried. The night and the sea were as dark and brooding as her heart . . . as fathomlessly, intensely, dangerously dark as Drake's ebony eyes.

At the clock's twelfth stroke they reached the island.

Thanking Dave, Ronnie was quick to hop from the Boston Whaler unescorted. As Drake watched her, her graceful, lithe cat movements, he felt a curious anger grow within him again.

She was once more cloaked in her cape of invincibility, her shield of marble ice. Following her up the path to the house, he felt his rage take on monstrous proportions. He wanted to shake her, to tell her to put on no airs around him. Damn it! He knew her. He knew her more thoroughly than any man alive, more thoroughly, he was sure, than the man who could rightfully claim her.

Something snapped in him as they reached the house and she set a slender, delicate hand upon the door. His arm shot out and he spun her around, nailing her to the wood with his body, pressing against her so that she was forced to adjust her form softly to his. Her eyes stared into his, naked for a second, startled and alarmed.

"Drake!" She whispered his name with beseechment, but neither knew if she pleaded for him to release her, or to carry out the action he couldn't control.

His lips were swift and harsh as they claimed hers, bruising and hungry. Her mouth had been parted and moist, and he found its plunder easy. She had no chance to resist, and his tongue drove deeply in demanding circular play that made response mandatory. She whimpered deep within her throat, and the sound brought out all that was primitive in Drake. His hands trailed her face and wove over her body, wedging space to cradle

111

her breasts possessively. His thumbs grazed over the nipples that had taunted him all night, and a savage satisfaction filled him as they rose instantly to his caresses. It was crazy; it was insane. He wanted to drag her into the garden, divest her of her garments, and gaze upon her exquisite marble beauty. She was his only, glowing with grace and majesty in the moonlight.

Drake ripped himself away from her as abruptly as he had wrenched her into the ruthlessly quick embrace. Ronnie stared at him, appalled, her knees buckling. Only the door kept her standing; only years of dignity kept her from quailing beneath the shocking ferocity of his dark scowl.

"Home, Mrs. von Hurst," he growled bitterly, bowing low with a terse mockery. "Once again, I thank you for a lovely time."

Ronnie pushed open the door and fled up the stairs, unaware that even her hasty exit was a regal, graceful sail and equally unaware that all of Drake's anger and mockery was directed at himself.

CHAPTER SIX

The simple task of rising and leaving her room the next morning was an arduous chore for Ronnie. Pieter, she knew, would not appear, and she would be left to face Drake alone. But she couldn't hide out all day, it would be cowardly. And God forbid, on top of everything else, Drake should call her a coward. . . .

Still, she stalled as long as possible, washing her hair leisurely, taking care to blow dry it. She showered for so long that she feared even their ample hot water supply would run cold, then convinced herself she needed a manicure and pedicure.

She was so perfectly primped, she told herself dryly, that she was like a young girl about to meet her lover. The thought brought a rush of miserable, ironic color to her cheek, and she quickly brushed it aside. Biting her lip, she knew she had to face the day, and Drake. Sweeping her hair into a severe knot, she finally opened the door and left her bedroom behind, hoping Drake had breakfasted early.

He had, but he was obviously waiting for her, drinking a second cup of coffee while he looked over the morning paper. As he spotted her entering the room he set the paper down and rose dramatically to greet her.

"Ahhh . . . my dear Mrs. von Hurst. Good morning."

The cynicism of his tone did little to improve her state of mind.

"Mr. O'Hara." She acknowledged him with a nod, hoping he didn't notice how tense she was as she glided past him to the sideboard. Her hands were steady as she poured herself a cup of coffee, and she decided toast was the most she was going to be able to stomach with his mocking gaze upon her.

He half lifted a brow as he reseated himself after solicitously pulling out and pushing in Ronnie's chair. "What happened to your appetite?"

"Not a thing," she said, stirring a spoonful of sugar into her coffee. "There are just days when I'm hungrier than others. Could I have a section of the paper, please?"

"Certainly."

Ronnie was careful to keep the print right side up as she accepted the front section. The news of the world, however, could not engross her, not when Drake was openly watching her with unfathomable eyes. Was he still angry this morning? He was sardonic, but not cruel; mocking, but not scornful.

It was best always to be on the defensive with Drake. Fairy tales were brief in duration.

"Did you have plans for the day?" Drake suddenly inquired.

She was taken off guard but answered quickly. "Yes. I'm behind in quite a bit of correspondence, and—"

"And I'm afraid you'll have to forget it." Drake grimaced ruefully and reached into his shirt pocket. Ronnie felt a queasy sensation as she saw him extract one of Pieter's monogrammed notes.

"What now?" she murmured skeptically. "We've already seen Charleston."

Drake pushed the note across the table to her. "Is this how you and your husband always communicate? You should hire a full-time postal clerk."

She stared at him while fingering the note, finding a dry, almost bitter humor in his eyes. "We don't need a postal clerk!" she snapped, unnerved by the note that promised another day in his company. He was dressed casually today, in dark pants and a white tailored shirt with rolled-up sleeves that not only accentuated his strikingly dark attractiveness and bronze tan, but emphasized the ample strength of his arms. God, it wasn't fair that anyone should tantalize so by mere appearance. She was tempted to reach out and run a finger down the exposed length of bronze flesh. During those magical days on the cruise she would have impulsively done so. But they were no longer on the cruise. Her fingers curled resolutely around her coffee cup.

"I suggest you read the note," Drake advised, ignoring her waspish tone.

Her eyes darted warily from his to the paper. They flew back to his with the panic she was too surprised and dismayed to hide.

Pieter's request for the day was ludicrous. He couldn't be serious. In her glance to Drake, she unwittingly pleaded and demanded agreement that it was so. But his eyes gave her nothing in return; they were enigmatically dark.

"I won't do it," she said with flat finality, pushing the note aside. In his very precise wordage Pieter "asked" that they spend the day working. He was worried about the marble pieces, so near completion, actually reaching that stage. Drake knew what he was doing, while Pieter's hands "troubled him."

To Ronnie's surprise, Drake shrugged with a casual lift of his brows. "Then that's that, isn't it?"

"Yes," she replied, more forcefully than necessary.

He took a sip of his coffee and leisurely lit a cigarette, watching her all the while, giving her the prickly feeling that she was being baited. "You sound as if you mean it," he finally commented.

"Well, of course I mean it," Ronnie retorted, annoyed. "I usually do mean what I say."

She saw the cynical arch of his brow too late. He had been baiting her, and she had fallen for the bait.

"Funny," he remarked idly, inhaling deeply on the cigarette, "I seem to remember you saying several things it appears you didn't mean."

What had happened to the warmth they had shared yesterday? she wondered fleetingly, carefully freezing her face into a mask of indifference so as not to allow him the satisfaction of seeing how deeply his barb had struck.

"Rest assured, O'Hara," she said coolly, "I do mean what I say this time." She did mean it. Posing for Drake and Pieter was mortifying. Posing for Drake alone would be unthinkable. She couldn't even think of a word to describe it. Suicide might be most appropriate.

He turned his attention back to his newspaper. "Whatever you say, Veronica."

He didn't believe her, she thought with annoyance. Well, this time he was going to learn a lesson about her willpower.

And he would have, she assured herself later with marked bitterness, if only it wasn't for Pieter. Without finishing either coffee or toast, she had left the dining room, only to find herself summoned to her husband's room.

If Pieter were really adept at something other than sculpture, that something was using and manipulating her. Looking pale and gray in the monstrous four-poster bed that seemed to consume him, he told her how much the pieces meant to him, how they might never be finished . . . unless she cooperated. He became so upset that, as usual, she backed down, concern overriding all other emotions. She was shortly assuring him that she would do anything in her power to help. And consequently, she was posing for Drake, her mind seething, her teeth sunk deeply into her lower lip.

Strangely, though, once she had admitted defeat with glacial quiet and and a dare in the lift of her shoulders and tilt of her head, Drake chose not to taunt her. He had known all along that she would be posing, and though her challenging reserve did not daunt him, he said little.

"Your husband is a difficult man to say no to," he had said simply when she sought him out.

And now, careful not to watch him as she arranged the drapery around herself, he said nothing. The room was deathly silent, and she instinctively knew that his dark gaze bored into her; she could feel the heat of his eyes. But he didn't come near her to make any adjustments as Pieter would have done; he simply waited.

Finally she could hear the grating of the chisel. Each rasp upon the marble was a cut across her nerves. In time, she was sure, she would toss back her head and emit a hysterical scream of pain. . . .

Drake was barely aware of what he was doing. His hands moved carefully upon the fine marble, but his eyes kept hazing over. Light beads of perspiration formed on his brow and threaded beneath his mustache, despite the comfortable temperature of the air-conditioned room. He paused several times to swipe at his forehead with the back of his arm and to nervously erase the moisture that clung to the fringe of black upon his upper lip. He was as miserable about the situation as she, but what did one say to a skeleton of a man whose eyes burned with fever as he pleaded?

He had lost to Pieter. He had known Ronnie would, and he hadn't meant to mock her this morning; he had meant to apologize. But his apologies meant nothing, and guilt and frustration drove him on, as well as the raging desire that burned him whenever she was near. . . . He really wasn't sorry that he had taken her into his arms. The sensation was too fundamentally right to be wrong . . . or to be denied.

He looked down at his fingers. They trembled, and he had to steady them before touching the delicate marble again. One mistake at this stage . . .

How long had they been working? He didn't know. A thin mist of perspiration was now breaking out across the backs of his hands. It was amazing, but the marble was taking shape beautifully . . . and the shape he carved was beautiful—slender, but so shapely. Sleek shoulder blades, the spine that curved exquisitely to tempting hips . . . and at the base of those hips would be the slightly indented dimples he had previously formed from sweet memory . . . agonized memory . . . memory that was driving him to a torture his mind could control, but his body couldn't handle. Flames were lapping at his insides, searing him, crippling him. . . .

She breathed, evenly and deeply. She could never be a "tool" to him. Each breath that caused the tiny motion of the expansion of the fine, shadowed lines of her ribs reminded him that she was not marble. She was warmth, fire, sweetness, unconquerable passion. . . .

Ronnie was reaching that point where she would scream insanely, like a demented shrew. The chisel grated, the chisel stopped. The silence between them was such that she could hear his every movement. The entire room seemed to have a life, that of his radiating presence, that of his heartbeats. . . .

The stillness was broken with a shattering impact when the chisel went flying across the room. Ronnie heard the strange whizzing sound, and jerked around quickly to see the tool crash into the far wall. Drake was staring at it with a disgusted look on his face, his hands planted on his hips. He glanced at her suddenly, aware that she was staring him. He didn't speak for a moment and offered no apology. "I think," he said finally, "that we have fulfilled our obligation. These pieces need only a few final touches—and Pieter should make those touches himself."

Ronnie nodded, only too happy to call it quits graciously. Drake had broken just seconds before she would have.

In her haste to scramble to her feet and escape the room, she stepped upon the long swath of silk drapery. The material jerked from her hands and fell to the floor, leaving her facing Drake totally naked.

She was too startled, too horrified, to make an instant grab for the material. It was not just her cheeks that suffused crimson; the color flooded her body from the roots of her hair to her pedicured toes. Still she didn't move; her eyes were held by a compelling prison of darkness.

It seemed like an eternity, but actually it was only seconds later that Drake came smoothly to her with a steady tread. He stopped directly in front of her, a semismile curving his lips. Crouching to his feet, he retrieved the drapery, rose, and carefully wrapped it around her shoulders. "Don't look as if the sky just fell," he said calmly, lightly tapping her chin with his knuckles. "I certainly didn't see anything I haven't seen before."

In mute misery Ronnie wrapped the material more tightly

around her, her clear sapphire gaze thanking him for the gentle kindness with which he had handled a moment he could have used to full advantage against her.

He did not linger near her but turned quickly to straighten the tools he had been using and to stoop and also retrieve the thrown chisel. "What's the story with that boat?" he demanded conversationally, as if nothing had ever happened and they were idly talking over afternoon tea.

The color was still receding from her body; her mind wasn't working quite as quickly as his. "What?" she murmured, disoriented.

"The boat," he said. "That Boston Whaler. Is it Dave's private property, or can I take it out?"

"Ah, no," she said quickly, rebounding from the incident. "I mean, no, the boat is for anyone's use. You're welcome to take her out. Just let Dave know you're going."

Drake wasn't looking at her, he was carefully covering the marble. "Want to join me?"

"What?" she murmured again, this time surprised.

"Damn, Ronnie," he said with a trace of amusement, "your eardrums must have turned to marble. I said, do you want to join me?"

"My eardrums are just fine," she assured him dryly. "It's simply that I find your invitation a shade peculiar."

"Why?"

"Why?" she repeated, amazed.

Drake laughed and looked around the room. "Is there an echo in here? I believe why was my question."

Ronnie sighed with exasperation and began to inch toward the door. "No, I don't want to join you. I want to avoid you as much as possible, and you know it, and you know exactly why. I don't think we make the most congenial of companions."

She had reached the door, and it appeared that he was advancing on her, but he wasn't. He reached for the knob. "Do you mind," he inquired politely. "I'd like to get by."

His acceptance of her refusal should have pleased her, but she felt curiously deflated. "Excuse me," she said, quickly stepping aside. Again she became disoriented.

Again she stepped on the drapery. And again it fell to her feet. She closed her eyes in rueful dismay, wondering bleakly why she should have chosen this day in her life to suddenly lose coordination. She felt Drake move to her feet and once more chastely redrape her.

Her eyes opened slowly. His were inches away, bright with laughter.

"If I didn't know better, Mrs. von Hurst," he said with dryly feigned chastisement, "I'd say you were trying to seduce me."

And she was doing a hell of a good job of it, he told himself. Far more beautiful than any statue ever created, the sight of her nakedness could tempt a cloistered monk. He knew her skin was like velvet. Even when frozen with dismay she stood proud, her breasts blossoming high and firm, her slender waist a handle of nature that knotted his fingers with memory. She was shadows, contours, curves, mystery, and enchantment. She was driving him nuts.

But she was as tormented as he was; he knew the trauma in her eyes so well. In spite of himself, he teased, he laughed, although the sound was a half guttural groan from deep in his chest.

She, however, did not find his teasing so amusing. He could see trauma simmering to anger. "Go on, Mr. O'Hara," she hissed, "you can get by now."

He felt his teeth grinding into his jaw. Damn her and her imperious reserve. Here he was, making light of a situation to save her feelings, and she was unsheathing her claws. "You first, Mrs. von Hurst," he drawled mockingly. "I'll make sure you get down the hall clothed."

"Please," she bit back, "it isn't necessary."

Drake didn't budge. Belatedly Ronnie saw by the hardening of his firmly squared jaw and the chilling intensity that swept into his eyes that she had made a mistake to snap at him. She was even dimly aware that her anger had been uncalled for. But

120

Mrs. von Hurst. The skirt drifted about her shapely legs like sheer mist while sporting a long slit that bared a glimpse of nyloned thigh when she walked—but again, she decided that Pieter would love it. Always the artist, his once purely aesthetic eye was now laced with warmth. He still appreciated a beautiful woman—even one he no longer called wife.

She slipped into a pair of matching heeled sandals, grabbed her evening bag and stole, and gave herself a final critical glance in the mirror.

Clothing and makeup, she thought with a sigh. They could do wonders. She looked fine, and when she smiled, she looked happy, which she was. Very happy for Pieter. He was eagerly looking forward to his new life.

She wanted him to believe she was happy, but she wondered if she ever could be again. Pieter did not hold her heart, but while he had needed her, she had cared for him and busied herself so industriously that she had managed to push her sense of loss to the back of her mind.

Tonight it was upon her full force. Drake had never really been hers, but she had been his completely. No matter how she tried to convince herself that a real love would come one day, she knew she lied. She was in love with a one-of-a-kind Black Irish devil. He would never come again.

A knock sounded at the door, and Ronnie focused her blurring eyes once more on the mirror to adjust her drooping smile. She wouldn't have Pieter see her with anything but the brightest face.

"Coming," she called cheerfully, spinning away from the full-length mirror and walking briskly to the door. She threw it open, and her heart missed a beat and seemed to stop entirely.

It was not Pieter at her door, it was Drake. She stared at him blankly for a moment, wondering desperately if she had conjured his image with sheer yearning. But she hadn't. No mere image could be as resplendent as Drake in a three piece, vested navy suit and elegant powder-blue French-cuffed shirt. Only Drake

164

despite the fact that the fault was her own, she had been humiliated, and humiliation could best be appeased by anger. Understanding the situation was going to do little to help her now.

"I insist, Mrs. von Hurst," he grated harshly, taking her elbow forcefully and propelling her out the door. "A lady should preceed a gentleman."

"I didn't know we had any present," she remarked beneath her breath.

He heard her. "Ladies, you mean?" He purposely misunderstood with a cutting, cynical tone. "Oh, come, Veronica. I would never refer to you as anything less than a perfect lady."

"Gentlemen," she retorted. "And I don't think I shall ever refer to you as one!" He was walking quickly, and she was breathless. It was difficult to keep up with his long-legged stride and keep herself wrapped to avoid any further disastrous mishaps.

He stopped at the door to her room and pushed it in before giving her a light shove inside. "I'll see you at the boat in thirty minutes," he said casually.

"You will not!" she promised, swinging the door shut only to have him prevent its closing with a quickly outstretched arm.

"Yes, I will," he said confidently. "We all know that Mrs. von Hurst does everything Mr. von Hurst orders."

Ronnie sucked her breath in sharply. He was observant; he was almost correct. But he was no better at denying Pieter than she was.

"What's the matter with you?" she retorted. "You have a will and a stubborn tongue—I can certainly vouch for that. You can say no. You should have today; you should have yesterday—"

"I didn't want to," he said simply.

"And anyway," she continued, her wrath rising, "Pieter did not tell me I had to go out on the boat with you. He asked me to work. I worked. I'm done. Finished. You go out on the boat if you want."

Drake wasn't sure himself what had gotten into him; she was right, they should stay far away from one another. But the anger he hated but could never quite control had him in its grip. He wanted to break her. He wanted to take her forcefully into his arms and make love to her with wild passion until she admitted she wanted him as badly as he wanted her.

He couldn't do that. He was stopped by his own morals as well as her denial. It was crazy—but then, he was a little crazy. Being in the house had slowly been driving him mad. He couldn't have her, but he wanted to be with her. Stupid and contradictory as it was, Drake was certain that she did love him in her way, and that that love would last forever.

As he looked at her, his face mirrored none of his feelings. It was hard, indomitable, ruthless. A devillike face—rawly handsome, sharply dangerous. Even more dangerous when he smiled slowly.

"You mean Pieter didn't ask you yet? It must have been an oversight. I'll go speak with him."

Ronnie really wasn't sure if he would go to Pieter, but she wasn't up to another meeting with him. It would be absurd. She would wind up promising anything. . . .

Soon, she promised herself, soon she would put her foot down. She won with him when she had the strength. More accurately, she won with him when she knew she was doing the right thing for his health.

Time was ticking by as she stared at Drake frigidly, indecisively. Why was he doing this to her? Didn't he realize how she loved just to be near him, to hear him talk, to watch him breathe? Maybe he did; maybe that was his way of tormenting her.

Yet she could have sworn that he had enjoyed yesterday as much as she had. He had held her as they danced with such genuine tenderness . . . but he had kissed her with repudiating violence. The best of their times together were destined to end that way.

Still, her choices were few. "I'll be at the boat in thirty minutes," she told him.

He made no effort to stop her as she slammed the door.

* * *

122

She had intended never to forgive him, and she hadn't really, she assured herself, as the Boston Whaler cut through the foamy indigo waves of the Atlantic. It was the sea that had broken the animosity between them; the swiftly changing depths of the mysterious ocean and the cleansing, healing salt wind.

It was impossible to be angry with anyone while speeding through the fascination of these elements. Especially when that someone was the devil's own spawn—a dark pirate at home in the wild winds, his angled, arrogant profile a dark bastion to challenge Neptune himself.

They had spoken briefly and curtly when they started out, but within fifteen minutes both were laughing gaily, recklessly. They spent an hour skimming over the open ocean in haphazard patterns, switching turns at the helm in unspoken agreement.

It was a glorious afternoon, hot for late summer in Charleston, but tempered by the relentless cool breeze that was part of the water sport. Drake had been farseeing enough to plan a basket lunch, but Ronnie was the one to suggest a sheltered alcove where the boat could be anchored while they ate their meal.

"No rocks!" Ronnie assured Drake as he watched her in silent doubt while she maneuvered the Whaler within twenty feet of the shore. "If she beaches, the tide will be with us. We can push her back out."

A moment later, with the anchor secure, Ronnie doffed the jeans she had worn over her bathing suit, rolled up the sleeves of her shirt, and hopped over the bow. The water, which came to her midriff, was delightfully cool after the heat of the sun. Shielding her eyes with a hand, she looked back to Drake. "Want to hand me the basket?"

He did, then hopped down beside her, holding a sheet procured from the cabin high above his head. Together they walked through the water to the beach.

"We're about a mile from where we brought the horses the other day," Ronnie remarked a little nervously. Drake hadn't said anything as he spread the sheet on the sand, and she was wondering if she should have suggested the alcove.

He nodded, looking down the beach. "That's about what I figured." He pulled his damp sport shirt over his head and tossed it to a corner of the sheet before taking the basket from her knotted fingers, setting it down, and sitting beside it. Rummaging through the interior, he found a cold-pack, unzipped it, and produced two bottles of Heineken. "Beer?" he queried her. "I hope it isn't too plebeian for your taste, but it seemed right for a boat excursion."

"It's fine," Ronnie said briefly, ignoring the mild taunt as she accepted the icy bottle. She seated herself on the other side of the blanket and once more bemoaned her impulsive suggestion. They had had no difficulty communicating aboard the Boston Whaler, but now conversation was stilted. They were also too close, too surrounded by primitive elements, and too near a state of undress. Drake now wore only a pair of cut-offs, and she wore only her rather skimpy bathing suit and the wet shirt.

She didn't move her head, but her eyes moved sideways. She wished she could ask him to put his shirt back on. He looked so much like that day she had first seen him by the ship's pool, casual but imposing, his bronze skin stretched tautly over a torso that was compellingly broad and sleekly muscled.

Ronnie looked quickly back to the sea. His savage kiss of last night seared her lips afresh with memory. His repudiation chilled her despite the heat of the sun.

"Why on earth did you insist I come with you?" she demanded suddenly.

He shrugged, and his eyes met hers. "I don't really know. But don't tell me you're not enjoying yourself. Your eyes light up like diamonds on that boat."

"You're capable of being charming on a boat," Ronnie admitted bitterly, digging her toes in to the sand. "It seems shorelines don't agree with us." She could feel herself winding up for an argument, and the prudent thing to do would be to find a sandwich and fill her mouth, but she couldn't control her harsh words. "Really, Drake. It amazes me that you find my behavior so atrocious. It never occurred to me that your type of man cared whom he sought for a rendezvous. I am not, after all, your wife."

"It's lucky for you, Ronnie, that you're not," Drake snapped scathingly.

"Really?" It was impossible to ignore such a blatant challenge no matter what the repercussions. "I suppose I would have been crucified by now?"

"Possibly."

"You'd condemn without a hearing?"

"I believe that marriage means fidelity."

So do I! she wanted to reply, but it would be ludicrous and laughable. "I suppose you had the perfect marriage yourself," she said derisively, immediately sorry that she had intentionally set out to wound him.

He stared at her calmly, but Ronnie intuitively knew that if his fingers hadn't been so tightly clenched around his knees, they would have been around her throat. "No, I didn't have the perfect marriage. I was only twenty-two at the time; rash and temperamental. We both took pleasure in outside flirtations when we fought, which was often. It was too late when we realized what we were doing to one another, how serious the games we played were. I swore when Lisa died that I'd never inflict such a relationship on anyone again—nor have it inflicted on me."

Ronnie could think of nothing to say to the direct reply she hadn't expected, but she didn't need to reply, she had gotten Drake going. His fingers left his knees to lash out for her arm, and she was dragged to the sheet so that he could heatedly stare over her, his weight half pinning her down.

"That's why I find your behavior so atrocious, Ronnie," he bit into her. "I spent fifteen years swearing I'd never marry again because it always involved games. Then I met you, and I believed you were guileless, completely sincere. You talked about love and forever. God, what a fool you made of me! Then I find out that you're not only married, but married to one of the greatest artists of our time. A man desperately ill. What were your promises for, Ronnie? Were you putting me on hold until Pieter kicked the bucket? That really wouldn't have been necessary, you know. I'm not worth quite what Von Hurst is, but my finances are fine."

Ronnie had remained stunned and still as he began his unleashed tirade, but the last was simply too much to tolerate. Where she had been chilled, she began to boil. She was shaking like a dry leaf in a winter wind. She exploded with a single word that well described what she thought of him, then went into a frenzied struggle against him. A worthless frenzied struggle.

His weight held her still and his arms fended her flailing limbs easily. He didn't even have to put forth much effort. He didn't speak, but smiled at her grimly until exhaustion brought her still again, panting, her eyes only challenging him with a blue ice that was as sharp as a glacier.

For several seconds she lay still, breathing, staring at his dark eyes. Then she twisted her lips into a smile as grim as his and sweetly hissed another sound expletive. "You're right, Drake," she finally told him, "absolutely right. I'd much rather be a widow wallowing in money than anyone's wife."

Drake released her roughly and stood, staring out at the sea, his hands planted on his trim hips. Ronnie watched his profile for a minute, cut sharply against the blue of the day, darkly rugged and uncompromising. Then she closed her eyes wearily. Nothing could change the facts.

Drake remained standing, watching but not seeing the sea and sky as he fought an inward battle for self-control. He didn't really know what he was after, except that he felt there had to be some sort of explanation. He wanted her trust. He wanted her to make him understand how she could have sworn such ardent love to him while knowing all along she would return to another man. He would so gladly understand, because in spite of everything, all logic, all absence of future, he loved her. He wanted to shake the truth out of her, but she didn't break, she didn't even bend. She tossed his accusations right back in his face. All he could do, he thought bitterly, was his best for her husband. His damnedest to restore that husband's health. Possibly restore her to his arms.

He couldn't really believe she was after the Von Hurst fortune. But then, why not? She had deceived him once into believing in forever. She could still be deceiving him—and Von Hurst. He was a fool to drown himself in the crystal-clear blue of her eyes.

Ronnie felt Drake's weight as he lowered himself back to the sheet. She flinched slightly and heard a mirthless laugh. "Relax," he told her dryly, "I'm not going to attack you with a ham sandwich."

She opened her eyes to find him collecting the beer bottles that had spilled into the sand while he chewed on a sandwich. "Your choices are ham and cheese and egg salad," he said brusquely. "Which will it be?"

"I'm not particularly hungry," she murmured, rising on an elbow.

He tossed a wrapped sandwich to her. "Eat anyway," he told her curtly. "I don't want you getting seasick on the way back."

"I don't get seasick," Ronnie protested as he handed her another beer.

"No," he said almost musingly. "I guess you wouldn't."

Was it a form of apology? Ronnie wondered. Perhaps the best he could do under the circumstances. Not an apology, she decided; at best, an armed truce. She began to chew her sandwich automatically. Let him lead the conversation; perhaps he could keep them off forbidden topics.

Halfway through a second sandwich he finally spoke, as if suddenly remembering that he wasn't alone. "I called my friend at Johns Hopkins after breakfast this morning. I'm going to talk to Pieter soon."

"What did your friend say?" Ronnie asked anxiously.

Drake shrugged, his brow furrowing into a frown. "There isn't a cure for his type of dystrophy, but it can be treated and controlled. There could even be a remission."

He hadn't been watching her as he spoke. He had given his

attention to the lettering on the beer bottle. Silence followed his last words, and he turned to her with tense curiosity.

Her eyes were brimming with tears that she fought to blink away. For the split fraction of a second before she could hide her emotions, Drake saw into her heart, and his anger melted away, replaced by that instinct that touched him to the core of his being—the instinct to care for and protect her. Logic and situation meant nothing; he was overwhelmed by the primordial, male urge to give his strength to the woman his senses claimed to be his own.

She drew away from him, her lashes fluttering furiously, her eyes wary and defiant. "Drake—" she protested, but she was in his arms, and once more, two forgotten bottles of Heineken were emptying into the sand.

"It's going to be all right, Ronnie," Drake murmured. "Pieter is going to be all right," he said with soothing conviction.

"Thank you," she whispered.

He had taken her to offer comfort. He knew it; she knew it. But suddenly the embrace changed. Neither would ever be able to say who instigated the change; it just happened. One second he was holding her shoulders, the next he was touching her hair. She had been limp in his arms; his touch revitalized her as instantly as a driven current of electricity. It was as basic as nature, as compelling as the ties that bound them together in a relationship that defied the outside world and even their own conscious thought. Seeds of love had been planted in both of them that flourished and grew despite themselves, despite everything.

As they touched they forged a private world. It consisted of the sea and sand and breeze around them, spiraling into a relentless whirl. The pounding of the surf became that of their hearts.

Drake's initial kiss, falling on moist lips that parted sweetly for his, brought them both back to the sheet. He could hear nothing but the provocative call of the surf, feel nothing but the touch of velvet that was her skin. He was a man possessed, and possessing what was his. Slender fingers tangled through his hair, draw-

128

ing him ever closer as his tongue probed her mouth for all its secrets, all its warmth. The hunger that raged within him could not be easily appeased, and his lips left hers to travel to her cheeks, her throat.

Ronnie shivered and moaned as the moist heat of his demanding kisses moved slowly down to her cleavage. The slightly abrasive rasp of his mustache teased her flesh unendurably; like him, she was aware of nothing except the force that drove them together. Her fingers left his hair to splay across his back, seeking with wonder the breadth of muscles that quivered beneath them. Her body curved to his, arched, a perfect, natural fit, hips melded to hips.

The roar of the surf pounded louder and louder, intoxicatingly filling their bloodstreams. Drake found the tie that held her bikini in place, and his fingers deftly released it. His tongue reached out to touch a roseate nipple with reverence, then his mouth moved in sensuous and heated command to claim it entirely. Fireworks shot off along the length of Ronnie's spine. She moaned as she shivered with the intrinsic delight, so absorbed with his essence and raw masculinity that his being even eclipsed the sun. Her lips fell to his bronze shoulder. Her teeth grazed it with abject longing as her fingers played along his spine, moving with assurance to his hips, and slipping beneath the waist of his cut-offs.

"I love you." She whispered the words without conscious thought. They were right, they simply came to her lips and muffled into his flesh. It didn't even register into her mind that she had spoken. . . .

But her tender plea was as strong a deterrent to Drake as a bucket of ice water thrown heedlessly into his face. His desire didn't lessen—not with the length of her supple, silky legs tangled with his and the warm, aroused peaks of her breasts pressed to him—but he was jolted back to reality. He had heard the words before.

A groan, guttural, harsh, and tormented, ripped through him with a violent shudder as he jerked himself away, leaping with one movement, like a panther, to his feet. His eyes tore into her as she lay in the sand, startled, then awareness filled her beautiful eyes, confusion turning to pain.

He had never seen her more lovely, her form a delicately curving, still-welcoming silhouette on the sheet. Stooping, he plucked her bikini top from its landing spot in the sand and tossed it back to her.

"Get dressed," he instructed, and though he meant his tone to be soft, it was curt and hard.

She rose majestically, her sable hair a cascade behind her, making no awkward, embarrased attempts to shield herself, but quietly redonning her garment with dignity.

Drake turned and strode for the water. He submerged himself in the salty depths, wondering acidly if steam rose above him. Surfacing, he strode vigorously along the shoreline, chastising himself with each movement for his lack of control. Guilt riddled him as he thought of Pieter. He was a guest in the man's house and was coveting his wife.

He had settled nothing with himself when he returned to shore and, consequently, barked curtly at Ronnie, who waited, regally calm, their things gathered together.

"Let's go," he rasped, dismayed at the violence still contained in his tone. He hopped aboard the Boston Whaler first, then jerked her arm with an oath when she attempted to ignore his overture of assistance.

Her eyes flashed as his arm brought her leaping over the side.

"Stop it, Drake," she charged him. "You're a hypocrite. Don't take it out on me when you're responsible for your own actions. I've never held a shotgun to your head and told you to touch me."

She was right. Coolly, calmly, regally right. It didn't make him feel one bit better, nor soothe his savage mood.

"It would be better if you had," he retorted coldly, at least in a semblance of control. "And speaking of hypocrites"—he arched a high, scornful brow—"I thought, Mrs. von Hurst, that *you* loved *your husband.*"

Ronnie blanched as if she had been struck. "I do," she said weakly.

"You bandy that word around a lot, madam."

"I don't bandy it about," she said tonelessly, turning from him. "I do love Pieter, and"—her voice became a whisper—"I do love you."

They were frigidly silent as they returned to the dock, keeping a safe distance of several feet between them that might have been miles, both riding the wind with a secret misery.

Drake seemed to have forgotten her completely as he moored the boat. He was so distant that she was shocked when his hand came to her arm to spin her around and into his arms before she could leave the deck.

"You're a witch, Mrs. von Hurst—a seductress, a temptress, a lying Circe." His fingers drove into her hair at the base of her neck, and he ravished her mouth quickly but with astonishing, intense demand. "But God help me, madam, I love you, too."

He hoisted her into his arms and set her on the dock, then released her to jump up himself.

He brushed past her, and his long strides swiftly put a breach between them.

Ronnie trudged more slowly to the house. His meaning had been perfectly clear. He loved her, but he despised her, too.

They both dined in their rooms that night.

CHAPTER SEVEN

Drake spent the following morning closeted with Pieter. Ronnie learned from Henri when she awoke that the two men had already been together for hours and that Pieter had left instructions that under no circumstances was he to be disturbed. He had requested, however, that she not leave the house.

"Thank you, Henri," Ronnie told the butler, turning her back to pour a cup of coffee from the buffet. She didn't want him seeing the ill-concealed unease the situation was causing her. Had Pieter summoned Drake, or had Drake insisted on an audience with his host? Whichever, she didn't like the idea of the two alone together for hours. No matter how she attempted to assuage her worry with self-assurances that Drake, knowing the truth of Pieter's condition, would say nothing to aggravate him, she simply couldn't control her nervousness. Drake had very strong beliefs as to right or wrong, and in his eyes she was wrong. They were both wrong. If Pieter was to press Drake, he might find it impossible to lie.

Morning became noon, and still neither man emerged from Pieter's suite. Ronnie gave up all efforts of pretending constructive industry in the house, and trailed upstairs to her room, halfheartedly agreeing to a tray when Gretel insisted she have some form of lunch.

Pieter and Drake were dining in Pieter's room.

After picking at her lunch, Ronnie settled herself in the fur comfort of her bed and forced herself to read a recently ordered novel. It was by an author she loved, and Ronnie usually found his books absorbing and engrossing. That day she went through the first chapter before realizing that the words had not congealed in her mind at all and that she had no idea of what she had read. Guiltily she set the book aside. It was too fine a novel to be fluffed through.

At least, she thought idly, she had killed more time. The digital clock on her dresser informed her it was past two. Surely the men would break soon, and she would know what was going on before she started climbing the manor walls or sitting on the bed like a child and screaming hysterically with frustration.

Restlessly prowling her room, she recalled for the zillionth time Drake's contrasting behavior each time they were together. He could be charming, occasionally kind. He could also be mocking and ruthless—all within seconds. He called her witch while claiming to love her.

But it was a love she couldn't—wouldn't—dare trust. She could stir his passions—savage, fundamental passions—but it was as if he despised her and scorned her even as he reached for her. . . .

Her hair received the brunt of her own ravaged pride and emotions. Thinking of Drake, she brushed the lustrous sable mass with a ferocity that was certainly beneficial to her scalp, if somewhat haphazardly. As her arm tired she chided herself—she had to settle down.

The secret meeting going on was a good one. Drake was going to convince Pieter to see the specialist he knew. Pieter would have hope. She should be ecstatic. But they had to be talking about more than a specialist. It had been hours . . . and hours. . . .

She stood perfectly still as she heard a knock at her door, wondering at first if wishful thinking had conjured the sound. But a tap came again, followed by Henri's tentative "Mrs. von Hurst?"

"Yes?" Ronnie flew to the door and flung it open expectantly, her hair falling about her face in thick, fluffy waves.

Henri stared at her blankly for several seconds and Ronnie,

having no idea in the turmoil of her mind that he was seeing her as he never had before, her face flushed, her hair wild, her manner reckless and impatiently vibrant, repeated herself anxiously. "Yes, Henri. What is it?"

Henri snapped his jaw back together, returned to the present, but still thought of his mistress with a new dawn of comprehension. She was young, beautiful, and spirited. Funny how the years of steadfast poise had always blinded him. Her rigid composure had made him think her far older, far more prepared to take on the desolation of the island and its inhabitants.

"Mr. von Hurst, madam," Henri said quickly, shuttering his thoughts with the rapid blinking of his eyes. "He requests you in his suite at your earliest convenience."

Ronnie laughed aloud, further startling Henri. Earliest convenience! Nice words for a command. Well, for once she and Pieter were attuned. Her earliest convenience was now! Even facing Drake after yesterday's stunning show of strange possession was preferable to enduring one more second of this awful, nerve-racking curiosity.

She didn't pause for an instant to check her appearance or bind her hair. With a brief nod of thanks, she swept past Henri, mindless that her gait was less than truly dignified as she sped down the corridor to Pieter's door and rapped on it briskly. She could hear the murmur of words from within, but a hush echoed to her after her first rap.

"*Entre!*" Pieter called, his use of the French word sounding almost studiously nonchalant.

Ronnie forced herself into a semblance of calm as she twisted the brass knob and pushed on the wood. The scene she came upon looked as if it had been purposely set. Pieter and Drake both sat in fan-backed chairs by the beveled window, comfortably leaning into the chairs, their legs crossed negligently.

They might have been discussing the weather, except that Ronnie knew better. There was tension in the fingers that rested on Drake's knee, an evasiveness in Pieter's light eyes. Yet oddly, Pieter seemed to be the happier of the two—almost complacent.

Drake was rigid . . . radiating that dangerous energy even as he sat. Ronnie covertly lowered her lashes to form crescents on her cheeks and watched Drake from beneath them. She caught a glimpse of his dark eyes and felt her breath depart her body. Unwitting chills assailed her.

He was furious. And, she realized as his arrogantly accusing stare came to rest upon her with explosive menace, it was not Pieter with whom he was furious. His wrath was directed at her.

Why? she wondered desperately. He had been angry yesterday, but surely not to this extent! Nor was there a hint of the yearning desire he had displayed yesterday despite his roughness . . . or the underlying core of a heated passion that burned with or because of the anger. . . . No. His wrath was brutally cold. It seemed to touch her like the tangible chill of an arctic wind. What could she possibly have done?

"Ronnie! My dear, you do remember Mr. Simmons, my attorney from Charleston?"

With one of his natural but dramatic hand gestures, Pieter motioned across the room, and Ronnie suddenly became aware that there was a third party in the immediate vicinity. She turned to the new guest, quickly hiding her surprise.

"Mr. Simmons, yes," she murmured graciously, extending her arm with a feigned pleasure. "How nice to see you."

Mr. Simmons was a dignified white-haired old charmer of legendary southern gentility. He accepted her hand with a slight squeeze and a small bow. "Dear Mrs.—von Hurst!" he replied in a low, modulated tone, "I assure you the pleasure is entirely mine." Ronnie noticed that he stuttered over her name.

Drake chose that moment to cough discreetly. Ronnie couldn't see him as she faced Mr. Simmons, but she could feel his scorn searing through her. She would have loved to politely excuse herself to Mr. Simmons and turn around and just as politely dump a bucket of ice water over Drake's head, or slap his mocking face, or, better still, drop him in a kettle of boiling oil. . . .

"Mr. Simmons has some papers for you to sign, Veronica,"

Pieter said, indicating his varnished rolltop desk. "Would you take care of it right away, please?"

"Yes, of course," Ronnie murmured automatically, pivoting to the large desk, her own bewilderment and curiosity quickly being replaced by a seething fury. Simmons must be there so that she and Pieter could legally fill out a marriage license. And Pieter, damn him, was nonchalantly carrying off this piece of very private business with Drake in the room. Had he let Drake in on their "family secret," or was his behavior so smooth that Drake would think it to be any document requiring both signatures?

Tears of humiliation were blurring her eyes, and she picked up the document to enable herself to read it, but her eyes refused to focus. A heavy band seemed to be constricting around her stomach, a band of inescapable steel that stopped her heart and closed in around her lungs. After signing this document, she would become Pieter's wife in truth. She had always claimed to herself and Pieter that the illegality of their original marriage had meant nothing.

But it had.

It had made it possible for her to spend that magical time with Drake—possible to grasp at interludes of happiness, and to dream and love.

There would be nothing faulty about the marriage this time. It would be legally registered in the State of South Carolina.

Pieter and Drake both rose simultaneously and came to her with swift strides—an amazing accomplishment for Pieter. Startled from her reflections, Ronnie dropped the document on the desk, her eyes widening with confused alarm as the two men seemed to swoop down on her like vultures. She emitted a little gasp as they neared her, and almost imperceptibly they slowed, and Pieter smiled. A quick glanced passed between him and Drake, and Drake changed course, walking across the room to Mr. Simmons—nowhere near her.

Had she imagined that he was coming for her? Ronnie wondered fleetingly. His change of direction had been so smooth. . . .

"Don't bother reading the thing, Veronica," Pieter instructed, securing a pen from the desk and slipping it in to her fingers. "I have more business to take care of, so I'll need you simply to hurry. And don't forget to use your, ah, proper name."

Proper name—maiden name. Uneasily Ronnie leaned over and signed Veronica Jane Flynn. Pieter immediately slid the paper from her and retrieved his pen, sighing. "That's that," he said with satisfaction.

Did the room reek of tension, or was she falling prey to the desolate life on the island and becoming paranoid? Pieter smiled at her benignly, Mr. Simmons casually glanced out the window, and Drake stood near him, quietly questioning him about growth along the Battery. Picture perfect. She *must* be growing paranoid. Drake had not been coming for her, he had just happened to rise along with Pieter.

With the document in his hand, Pieter suddenly seemed to wilt before her. The normal pallor of his face took on a gray tinge, and for a moment Ronnie feared he would crumple to the floor. Ronnie forgot all the peculiar behavior surrounding her; she even forgot that Pieter usually shrugged off her touch sharply. She gripped his arm with naked concern, supporting him.

"Thank you, my dear," he murmured. "I think I do need a little help over to my chair."

He had spoken softly, but Drake was at his side in a minute, nodding to Ronnie over his head with unspoken instructions in his eyes. Together they led Pieter back to his chair by the window.

"Thank you," Pieter murmured again.

Once more Drake's eyes met Ronnie's. The mutual agreement they had shared so swiftly in regard to Pieter was gone. The hostility was back. Burning, scorching hostility. The look was deadly, but she couldn't seem to tear her eyes away from the flame. Thankfully Mr. Simmons broke them apart.

"I think that's all that I need," the older man said cheerfully, taking the paper from Pieter and placing it in his neat nondescript briefcase. "Mr. von Hurst"—he shook Pieter's hand—"I'll return in three days. Mrs. von Hurst, if you'll escort me out . . ."

"Certainly," Ronnie replied, "Pieter? . . ."

"You'll come right back here, please," he commanded.

"Excuse me," Drake interrupted. "Perhaps I should see Mr. Simmons out. I'm sure that whatever you have to say to your wife must be personal, and I can leave you two alone now—"

"No!" Pieter protested firmly. "I want you here, Drake."

Ronnie was surprised by Pieter's vehemence, and stunned by his words. She felt an uncomfortable coldness implacably settling in her limbs. Pieter hadn't wanted her to read the paper. What in hell had she just signed?

"Pieter." Drake set his jaw with the protest. "I don't think—"

Pieter lifted a hand weakly, and Ronnie had a slow dawning, and astounding suspicion, of what was going on. He was feigning part of his illness now, using it deviously to manipulate Drake. He knew the other man—the stubborn, indomitable, Black Irishman—had a will to fight anything, except his weakness.

"Drake, please," Pieter insisted, and if she didn't know him better, Ronnie could have sworn he hid a satisfied smile. "Mr. Simmons is waiting, Veronica."

"Yes," Ronnie said, challenging him with a hard stare. "Yes, I'll be right back. Mr. Simmons . . ."

She exited the room politely with the lawyer and waited until they were halfway down the staircase before turning to him bluntly. "Mr. Simmons, what did I just sign?"

Brilliant color flooded the older man's face, and he began to stutter. It was obvious he hadn't expected the question. He lowered his head and hurried down the remainder of the stairs, stalling for time.

"Mr. Simmons," Ronnie persisted, keeping pace with him as he stretched his strides to reach the door. "You are an attorney, sir. I believe I have just put my signature upon something important without proper legal counsel."

"Mrs. von Hurst—Veronica." Simmons still seemed to be fumbling with her name, but then he was aware of the circumstances. "Please speak to your husband. To—uh—Pieter."

Ronnie sighed with exasperation. "Can you answer me one question, *please?* Is Mr. O'Hara aware of anything?"

"Oh, no, no!" Simmons was able to assure her. "I just arrived —I drew the papers up long ago. Mr. von Hurst summoned you for your signature as soon as I entered the room."

Ronnie was sure from Simmons's conspiratory and sympathetic look that he was placating her for all the wrong reasons. He imagined that she found her invalid marriage a horrifying embarrassment; after all, she had been living with Von Hurst for five years, a situation not actually shocking in the society of the eighties, but still not entirely palatable to the Bible Belt of the Old South. She hid a dry smile. She was far too concerned about Pieter to give a damn about propriety, but Simmons couldn't possibly comprehend her feelings. He could imagine what he wanted.

But if Drake knew nothing about the paper, why had he jumped to prevent her from reading it? She hadn't imagined his action—it wasn't paranoia.

Simmons, awed by the straightforward, cool confidence of the elegant young woman, suddenly found himself spilling far more than he intended. "I assure you that the document is in your best interests and protects you completely. I admit, Mr. von Hurst did plan to trick you, and that he did ask Mr. O'Hara's assistance. . . ." Simmons's voice trailed away inaudibly. Von Hurst was the main client of his office—the main income. He wasn't to be offended, and if that had meant joining in a small deception . . . Oh, well, *he* hadn't stopped her from reading the paper. . . .

"Mr. Simmons," she charged him bluntly. "That was not an application for a wedding license, was it?"

"No," he murmured unhappily, praying she would ask him nothing more.

139

She didn't. "Thank you for that much honesty. Good afternoon."

Very unhappily Simmons left the house and started down the path for the Boston Whaler, his ticket off the island.

Ronnie watched him for several seconds and then turned with forceful steps to the staircase. It was time for a confrontation, and she was ready to battle Pieter. There would be no more humoring.

She charged into Pieter's room without knocking, startling both men who awaited her. Casting a quick, hostile glance at Drake, she turned the flow of her force to Pieter. Her voice was a low, controlled growl. "I insist on knowing what is going on here!"

Pieter smiled. "I'm divorcing you, Ronnie."

His reply momentarily stunned her. How could he be divorcing her when he knew they weren't really married?

Then she understood completely. Somehow, *Pieter knew.* He knew that she was in love with Drake, and was determined to play matchmaker. This announcement in front of Drake was a show. The tides were changing again. Pieter was trying to take care of her, at his own sacrifice. She loved him for it, but she couldn't let him do it. Tears misted in her eyes as she approached him, facing him squarely. "No, Pieter, I simply won't let you do it."

He turned from her, and in his life he had never been more callous. He had to be. "I'm afraid you have no choice, my dear. You have just signed a document absolving me of any responsibility for you. I will be leaving shortly for Maryland and this Johns Hopkins doctor Drake has arranged for me to see. I want you off the island before I return."

Ronnie knew Pieter; she knew what he was doing and her heart went out to him. Nobility fit him well.

Drake gasped, and Ronnie cast him a quick glance. He didn't know what was going on. His countenance was brilliantly hard, his eyes laser-sharp diamonds. He was seeing the great Pieter von Hurst cruelly strip his wife of everything. "Pieter," he began harshly. "Lord, man, this is extreme. What we had was a brief affair . . . the woman really loves you."

It was Ronnie's turn to gasp. Drake had told Pieter about their shipboard romance.

"Oh, God! Pieter!" Tears streamed down Ronnie's face for the man she had called husband, the man she had hurt so badly, who was now staging this whole thing for her benefit, not realizing how Drake despised her for the affair to begin with . . . and how she despised him now for the pain he had caused with his admission. She rushed to the huge fan-backed chair in which Pieter had wearily sat. "I'm so sorry, Pieter," she cried, clasping his terribly gaunt hand once again with no thought of being rejected. She caught his sad blue gaze, strong now with his determination, and her tears continued in a waterfall torrent. She couldn't stop them. "Pieter," she choked, "you still can't do this, I won't let you. . . . Oh, Pieter . . . you can't. I know that you need me. . . ."

He looked at her with love and tenderness. "No, Ronnie. No more."

Drake couldn't see his host's eyes, only the humble tears in Ronnie's. And he was furious. Von Hurst had tricked him into admitting the affair, smoothly bribing him. He would go to Johns Hopkins only if Drake would accede to the fact that he was in love with Pieter's wife. And with the admission necessary to offer the great artist life, Drake had felt his rage rise at Ronnie, who had deceived him from the beginning. Ronnie, who had no life with Pieter . . . Ronnie, who had sworn her love for him. . . . Ronnie, who, now offered complete freedom—no, forced into complete freedom—was groveling at the feet of the man who had callously cast her out. Good God, he was being used by both of them! But what hurt him most was the fact that she didn't turn to him. He couldn't love her as Von Hurst's wife, but if Von Hurst was sworn to repudiate her . . . she should accept it. Supposedly she loved Drake, too.

Drake could literally feel his heart harden. He had been deceived all along. Ronnie cared for Pieter, desired him, but really gave her love to no one. There could be only one reason that she pleaded so fervently with Pieter: She liked being Mrs. von Hurst. She couldn't part with the prestige and promised wealth.

She was still crying, and oddly, Von Hurst was trying to soothe her. "I know what I'm doing," he told her.

"Oh, Pieter" was all that she could mumble. She stumbled to her feet, still murmuring, "No, I won't let you. . . ."

Then, with her beautiful sapphire eyes glinting like a multi-faceted crystal chandelier, Ronnie turned a weary, scorning gaze to Drake. The air between them was thick and charged with tension.

She was angry enough to stare Drake down, angry enough to meet his contempt—angry enough to really boil him in oil, if only she had a big enough pot.

But she also felt as if she were bleeding within, and the room was closing in on her. She couldn't bear any of it anymore. Ripping her eyes from the electricity of Drake's, she strangled a sob and raced out of the room, down the staircase, and out of the house.

Both men were silent for several minutes after she left the room. Drake began to pace, running his fingers through the raven wings of his hair. Damn Ronnie! How could she have put him in a position like this? Morally, he was bound to argue that the man keep his wife—a wife Drake's heart felt to be his.

"Damn it, Von Hurst!" he finally exploded. "I don't think you understand Ronnie—"

"I understand her perfectly, O'Hara," Pieter responded. "And I understand you, my friend." Pieter sighed wearily. He was not all that good at being generous. It was becoming harder with the two of them fighting him. "Always follow the command of your heart, Drake. There is a season in life for everything. In this season of my life I am following my heart."

"Von Hurst," Drake began heatedly, "if you're following your damn heart, keep me out of it! You used me today—"

"Yes." Pieter waved a hand that was truly growing weak. Watching the younger man was tiring. He was a panther on a

142

leash, exuding vitality, restraining himself. Von Hurst knew Drake would love to bash his fist in his face. He also knew he wouldn't do it.

"Would you go find . . . Veronica, please," Pieter requested. "I do not want her alone." His wife. His dearly beloved wife. He would never use the term again. "You will find her by the sea. She has probably taken one of the horses."

Drake stormed out of the room gladly. He wasn't sure it was such a good idea for him to find Ronnie at that moment, but it wasn't a particularly good idea for him to stay with Pieter. In his present mood he wanted to throttle them both. He felt like a volleyball they had been passing back and forth, and for the life of him, he couldn't begin to figure out what the hell was going on. He had spent the morning convincing Pieter that he should see another doctor. Pieter then had charged him very politely with having an affair with his wife, never once losing his temper. To the contrary, he had seemed pleased. . . . He had assured Drake then that he would see the doctor. Then he had become excessively weak and begged Drake to help him force Ronnie's hand, and then the attorney had appeared. Then Pieter, who hadn't even been angry, was telling his wife he was divorcing her . . . then . . .

The entire situation was mad, and he couldn't even get out of it. He was too involved—and too much in love, as well as frustrated, confused, and terribly furious—and suddenly, very, very determined to find Ronnie. They were going to have it out once and for all.

His fists clenched into iron vises at his sides, Drake stalked down the stairway in pursuit.

CHAPTER EIGHT

Pieter did know Ronnie much better than she would have ever guessed.

Her first instinct was to run to the stables and to the bay mare. Startling the elderly groom, she slipped a bridle over Scheherazade's head herself and shunned the idea of a saddle, grasping the mare's mane to swing herself astride in a reckless but practiced leap.

Her second instinct was to race to the sea. She followed the trail through the lower foliage until she broke out on to the beach. There she gave Scheherazade free rein, and allowed the pounding of the surf and the horse's thundering hooves to drown out the throbbing in her head.

Finally Ronnie realized she was overtaxing the mare, and she reined in. Scheherazade slowed obediently and came to a halt.

Ronnie slid from the horse's back and walked numbly to the water's edge, heedless of the waves that saturated her loafers, washing over them like slender, receding tentacles. She sat and lay backward, throwing an arm over her eyes to shield them from the sun.

Not since Jamie's death, so many years before, had she been at such a loss. And not in the five years of their pseudomarriage had she ever felt closer to Pieter. Yet never in her life had she encountered the love she felt for Drake—an emotion that overwhelmed all else, including her own will.

It was such a fiasco. She knew damn well that Pieter would never force her off the island, and she also knew, no matter how noble his gestures, that he would need her to endure the trauma of once again searching for hope.

She felt the approach of Black Satan reverberating in the sand even before she heard the sound of his galloping hooves, and she winced. She was in no mental condition to do battle with Drake.

Twisting her head and covertly opening an eye beneath the shade of her arm, she watched with an almost detached admiration as the horse and rider came nearer. Black Satan, huge, powerful, and magnificent stallion, like a war horse of another era, thundered down the beach. His rider was equally powerful, equally magnificent. As if it had been staged, Drake was in black today: black jeans and a black silk shirt, with sleeves that rippled in the wind. Drake too had shunned the use of a saddle, and he seemed to sail down the beach, one with the stallion. A black knight.

So much for Cinderella tales, she told herself grimly. She would have laughed if she didn't fear the laughter would turn to hysteria. This was certainly no fair prince coming to wipe out the misery of the past with a single kiss of loving tenderness. It was Drake, his dark, brooding scowl a countenance as foreboding as his appearance. She could already see the dangerous gleam of anger glinting like black diamonds in his eyes.

He wasn't coming to give her a tender, loving kiss.

The stallion came to a rough halt about thirty feet from her. Drake was off the horse's back in an instant, his long strides carrying him swiftly to her. He gripped both her hands with thin-lipped determination and jerked her curtly to her feet, releasing her as she stood. Ronnie automatically rubbed sore wrists as she stared at him, inwardly strengthening herself as she noted the harsh irregularity of his breathing as he glared at her.

They stood like that for several seconds, just staring at one another, both unaware of the sea that foamed over their feet or the horses that wandered aimlessly in the background.

Drake finally spoke as he saw her chin begin to tilt. Even now, with her sable hair whipped by the wind and her jeans and tailored shirt spattered with water and wet sand, she was regal.

"I want to know," he grated harshly, his words enunciated crisply between the clench of his jaw, "what the hell is going on here."

Ronnie shrugged with cool eloquence. "Why are you asking me? You seem to be privy to more information than I. You also seem to be giving out more."

"I didn't tell Pieter a damn thing he didn't already know," Drake growled with low menace.

"But you did tell him something?"

"I had to."

Ronnie did laugh then, a short, bitter sound. "You once told me, Mr. O'Hara, that I did everything my husband instructed. How does it feel to find yourself in the same position?"

It was the wrong question. Ronnie gasped with alarm as Drake's hands came to her shoulders, gripping them with barely controlled intensity. His eyes were a dark, savage fire as they seared into hers, seeming to scorch her soul. "I'll tell you how I feel," he clipped. "Used. Used in some travesty between the two of you. You were terrified that your husband would discover your little indiscretion. Because of his health, so you tell me. Well, I don't wish to blatantly insult you, madam, but your husband seemed ridiculously happy to hear about your outside affairs. He seemed thrilled for a good excuse to get himself an easy divorce.

"Now, on the other hand"—his pressure on her shoulders increased as he pushed her back to sit in the sand and crouched before her, barely losing a beat in his dissertation—"I have you. You claim to love your husband, but you weave me into your little spell at the same time. I'm supposed to believe that you will do anything, sacrifice all, for the husband you so adore, while carrying on with me as if I were some sort of a stud service—and, oh, you forget to tell me the conditions!"

His words had finally gone past the boundary of endurance. She instinctively followed one of the oldest impulses of time and slapped him with every ounce of seething strength she could muster.

146

He appeared almost not to notice. He stopped for a single second, procured both her wrists with a not-too-gentle wrench, and continued speaking. "Now we have our bountiful little princess of charity faced with a divorce from a man she is benignly staying with because he is an invalid. A man she couldn't possibly have slept with for some time. A man who wants nothing more to do with her."

"Let me go!" Ronnie hissed.

"Uh-uhn, princess. You're going to hear this one out. Then you're going to do some talking."

Ronnie made one quick attempt to extract her wrists from his grip, and then realized the futility of the effort. She went motionless, closed her eyes, and ground her teeth together.

"There really is only one deduction that can be made here," Drake went on, his tone still harsh and bitingly academic. "Mrs. von Hurst may enjoy an occasional excursion into the carnal delights of life, but she is very fond of being Mrs. von Hurst. Luxury is easy to become accustomed to, even though our magnanimous lady claims she also loves me—our third party in this little drama. Being the humble lover, I even tried to convince Mr. von Hurst that a divorce was a bit drastic—that his beautiful wife found me merely a diversion and was still deeply in love with him. But I failed, madam. Your husband is cheerfully determined to be rid of you. He will get a divorce."

"You are an idiot!" Ronnie hissed explosively. "A complete fool."

"Obviously," Drake drawled, "I'm involved in this. But be thankful you did involve yourself with an idiot. No matter what Pieter does," he added with a bitter note, "I will take care of you."

Ronnie laughed again. It was all so ridiculous. "Don't be absurd, Drake!" With his scorning attitude she'd die before he ever took care of her. "I repeat," she charged, her sapphire gaze challenging his dark one as she made a rash, foolish attempt to free herself, which only served to tighten his constricting hold, "you are an idiot. That entire scene in Pieter's room today was staged. I can guarantee you, my dear Mr. O'Hara, that I will never need you to take care of me. Pieter will not throw me off the island. Nor will he divorce me. He can't divorce me, because we're not really married."

Shock did for Ronnie what all her struggles could not. Drake's hands went cold and limp; his bronze face went paper-white beneath the tan. In contrast, his eyes became blacker than the night, his mustache and hair perfectly etched lines of ink against parchment. The reddening imprint of her hand became clear against the high, angular line of his cheekbone.

"What the hell are you talking about?" he rasped.

"Pieter and I are not really married," Ronnie repeated furiously. She was no longer in the least bit numb, but in the full heat of a long-withheld rage herself. She jumped to her feet, still careful to put a little distance between Drake and herself. "I told you, that entire scene was staged for your benefit. I suppose Pieter used the term *divorce* because he was afraid you would think less of me for living with him for all these years. It's a pity the poor man doesn't realize there is no way you could possibly think any less of me."

She had moved down the beach as she delivered her stunning retort, hoping to escape the touch that sent shivers down her spine even as it imprisoned her with demand.

But there was no escaping him today. He was on his feet with agile, lightning speed, and by her side to grasp an arm. "Don't walk away from me, Veronica—you're far from done."

"The hell I'm not!" she asserted. "You seem so great at judging everything. You take it from here!"

"Sit, Ronnie," he grated, "or shall I help you?"

She hesitated just a moment too long, which was foolish. She knew he never made idle threats. A slight movement of one of his powerful thighs swept her feet from beneath her and she was in his arms, being lowered back to a sandy seat. Just to be certain she didn't move again, Drake crooked an elbow over her waist and settled his head into his hand. His weight was held off her, but it was a very effective prison nonetheless. There was no way she could move the bar of his arm or push past the broad chest that hovered in front of her. "I'm listening," he reminded grimly as she stared at him, silently seething.

"All right, your honor," she grated mockingly. "But you're not going to understand—"

"I'm dying to understand," he interrupted dryly. "Try me."

Ronnie sighed and clenched her eyes shut for an instant. It was ridiculous, but in the midst of all this, her fingers itched to reach out and touch the crisp, smattering strands of black curls that rose above the two open buttons of his silk shirt. She was tempted to draw a tender line along that of the mustache that could quirk with his laughter, tease her flesh with exotic torment. . . .

Her eyes flew open. They met the relentless dark glare of his.

"Pieter and I were married in Paris as I told you," Ronnie said. "We came here right after—Pieter didn't want to be seen anymore. It was very rough on him at first, as you can imagine. He was impossible for a long time, but—contrary to what you believe—I did love him. Maybe not in a way you would condone, but I did and do love him. About a month ago he went into a period of brooding, and I finally learned it was about me. He got this thing in his head that he had ruined my life and he wanted to give me a divorce so that I could have a life of my own. He contacted his attorney, and consequently discovered that our marriage wasn't valid, because the notary who had performed the ceremony wasn't a notary at all." She smiled dryly. "He wanted a secret ceremony to avoid the press, and it was so secret, it wasn't even real."

"Go on," Drake prodded briskly as she fell to silence.

"That's about all there is to tell," Ronnie said blandly, focusing on the waves behind Drake rather than on his eyes. "I told Pieter from the beginning that I wouldn't leave him. Whether we were or weren't married was irrelevant. I consented to be his wife in Paris because I knew that he loved me, and he needed me very desperately. I don't think that that has changed. Pieter has sim-

149

ply decided that I want you, and he is determined to give you to me."

Drake became the still one. He was silent for so long that Ronnie forced her gaze from the sea back to him. She became aware of a chill as she watched his face, and she wasn't sure if it came from the damp sand and her soaked feet or not. He had regained his color, and he was in complete control now of his actions. The face she stared upon was hard and implacable, darkly grim, giving away nothing.

"You knew you weren't married at the time of the cruise," he finally said. His tone was no more readable than his face. Did he intend to forgive her on a legality? She couldn't allow such a falsehood.

"I knew about the marriage being invalid," she said bitterly, forcing herself to meet his demand squarely without tears forming in her eyes. "But"—her voice grew hard with the effort to be cold—"don't go absolving me of adultery or 'game playing,' as you call it. Whether that marriage in Paris was legal or not, I entered into it with wide-open eyes. I made all the vows. So you see, to me, I was married. I was Mrs. Pieter von Hurst."

"Then why me?" he asked hoarsely.

Ronnie swallowed carefully, and despite herself, she could answer in no more than a strained whisper. "I—I never intended there to be a you. Pieter forced me to take the cruise—you are right; he can use his illness to get just about whatever he wants— because he assumed a taste of freedom would make me agree to allow him to die alone. He feels the end is near." She had to stop for a minute to breathe deeply in order to continue without sobs choking in her throat. "When I met you, I thought we would share a drink. I knew what I was coming home to, and knew that no matter what Pieter did, I couldn't just walk out on him. I never thought I would see you again. And I—and I—" God, it was so hard to explain! "I just wanted you so badly." Her voice wasn't even a whisper, it was a feeble gasp for air.

Drake lifted his head and straightened himself, releasing her from the prison of his body. She stared at the sea; he stared at the cliffs. His long, strong hands moved to his face, and his fingers tiredly massaged his temples.

"How many other 'cruises' have there been?" he asked obliquely.

The question should have made her angry, but it didn't. Her anger was spent; her heart was torn in pieces.

"No other cruises, Drake. That was it."

He still wasn't looking at her and he asked his next question almost absently. "Do you really love me, too, Ronnie?"

Her throat constricted completely. He had stripped her veneer, plundered the depths of her life. It would be foolish to lie now, foolish to hold on to any false pride. Things were out in the open now, but they hadn't changed. Nor did she feel Drake's basic beliefs could change. Of her own admission, she had carried on an affair while still being, in her own mind, a married woman. It was a vicious circle. She couldn't leave Pieter despite his noble gestures; Drake would never trust her, even if she could leave Pieter. So none of it mattered . . . except that it did. She did love Drake with all of her heart, and now she couldn't bear a lie between them. Soon enough the time would come when she would never see him again.

"Yes." All of the warmth and yearning of the love she bore him came out in the barely audible whisper of the word.

Drake rose to his feet, a little unsteadily. He continued looking out at the cliffs, his profile as ruggedly indiscernible as the terrain he surveyed. He didn't soften, he offered her no tenderness.

He turned back to her and grasped her hands almost as roughly as he had originally. She came to her feet, and only then did his eyes meet hers.

"I'm going to marry you, Ronnie," he told her in a voice that was devoid of any emotion.

"No," she murmured in confusion. "You still don't understand. You can't."

He shrugged, peculiarly remote. "Yes, I can," he said distantly, "and I intend to."

Ronnie shook her head, her brows knit in confusion, her teeth nervously chewing the tender flesh of her lower lip. She was sure he had lost his senses, but he portrayed nothing to her now, not anger, not mockery, not sympathy, not love. He spoke with the absent courtesy of a casual acquaintance.

"You're not listening, Drake," Ronnie said firmly. "When Pieter leaves for Maryland, I'll be with him. I can't leave him to face hope—and possible disappointment—by himself. I will be with him."

Drake ignored her and let loose a shrill whistle. Black Satan obediently left the outcrop of grass he had discovered and trotted to the man, as acquiescent as a well-trained and beloved dog.

Soul mates, Ronnie thought with a shade of resentment for both man and animal. The fiery horse and arrogant man did deserve one another.

Drake swung over the stallion's back with expert ease. "Where's Scheherazade?" he asked her curtly.

Ronnie searched the area quickly with a sweep of her eyes. Her resentment for Drake's charismatic influence over the usually aloof Black Satan increased as she realized she had been deserted by Scheherazade—an animal she had owned for five years.

"Probably back at the stable, munching sweet alfalfa," she answered in annoyance.

"Then you'd better hop up," Drake suggested, sliding back to give her room over the horse's withers.

Ronnie stared at him uneasily. He hadn't responded to her announcement that she would be leaving with Pieter; in actuality, he hadn't responded to much of what she had said at all.

He had given her his bland yet determined offer of marriage, and then nothing else. He had ignored her commitment to stay with Pieter. Probably because he preferred it that way, she thought with dry misery. He might now believe that she did love him, and he might even still love her in return, but he didn't really want marriage. It was probably a moralistic, noble gesture —the type Pieter was proving to be so proficient at.

She was back to her vicious circle, and suddenly just as happy as Drake to drop the subject, which had so recently overshadowed all else. She wasn't, however, very happy to mount the black stallion with Drake. She was drained and more vulnerable than she would ever have him see her.

He held the reins with one hand and offered her the other. "Mrs. von Hurst—" He caught himself. "But that isn't your name, is it? What is your surname?"

"Flynn," Ronnie murmured, touching his hand but not accepting it. "I, uh, can't jump up that way," she explained with lowered lashes. "Black Satan is a lot higher than the bay—"

"Take my hand," Drake interrupted impatiently.

She did so and was surprised to find herself lifted high enough to swing a leg over the animal's neck and shoulders, in front of Drake. Careful of Black Satan's comfort, she scooted back to unnerve her own well-being. She fit like a glove to Drake's body, and was able to feel the slightest twitch of his muscles, from his strong thighs to the shoulders that sheltered her back. She could feel the expansion of his broad chest against her flesh with each breath, the thud of his heart. She could almost feel the racing of his blood through his veins. . . .

"Ready?" he queried crisply.

She nodded, and he nudged the stallion toward home. Black Satan, knowing the direction indicated offered a meal, tossed his huge, well-sculpted head, snorted, and attempted to take the bit between his teeth.

Drake was ready for him, clearly the master, but he allowed the horse a fleet canter. Ronnie clamped on to a handful of the sleek black mane, her thighs, like Drake's behind them, holding Satan while they moved with him.

Drake's arms were around her as he held the reins, loose but secure. She and Drake were one, and one with the horse. The wind whistled by them, the sun splayed down upon them, and the scent of the sea filled their senses.

Her life was a fiasco, but as they rode, Ronnie shared a brief, intimate pleasure with Drake. She realized poignantly how very much alike they were. They were both attuned to the joy of the wind, of the animal beneath them, of the wild and voluptuous summer beauty of the craggy island. And no matter what the tumult was between them on a mental or verbal level, they would always find harmony in their bodies, a rhythm that claimed them as they rode, a rhythm that would claim them eternally in one another's arms. . . .

Drake brought the stallion to a trot as they broke the trail foliage on the return and approached the stable. Ronnie became even more acutely aware of the perpetually strong and secure arms that held her, of the heartbeat she knew better than her own, of the delicious scent that was uniquely his, as crisp and clean as the sea, as enticing and enigmatic as the wind. A scent entirely masculine. . . .

The ride was over. The house loomed before her like a luxurious monstrosity. But she couldn't blame the house; the chains that bound her existed in her own heart and soul.

Suddenly she couldn't bear another second with Drake touching her, so close, yet miles out of her reach. The days they had shared before in tentative friendship and disastrous discord had been shattering. She needed time to mend the cracks that were threatening to tear down the facade of indomitable marble she must have to maintain her existence.

Black Satan stopped a few feet from the watering trough. Ronnie pushed Drake's arm aside and slid from the stallion, just catching herself from stumbling.

She didn't look back at Drake but turned her steps toward the house. Drake made no attempt to stop her. She could hear him vaguely as he talked to the groom. The bay had indeed returned and was safely in her stall. Mr. von Hurst, having heard the horse had returned riderless, was beside himself with worry.

Ronnie sighed with a breath that trembled. Drake could go and assure Pieter that she was fine. She had had it for the time being. Both of the willful men who tried to manipulate her life could go hang.

She was a mess, mentally and physically. Bareback riding had left her jeans covered with bay and black hairs and the damp

154

lather of the horses. Her feet were cold and aching from the wet shoes, and she was splattered with seawater and sand.

A long, hot, revitalizing bath was in order.

Despite her dishevelment she was able to sail coolly by Henri with a brief greeting of acknowledgment. "Mr. von Hurst is quite concerned, madam . . ." the butler called after her as she glided up the stairs.

Ronnie paused a second, her hand barely touching the banister. "Mr. O'Hara will see Mr. von Hurst," she answered calmly, wondering idly what Henri was going to think of her grimy footprints on his shiny wood floors. "I'll be in my room," she added firmly, never more than now the mistress of the house. She started walking again, then, aware that he watched her in puzzlement, she turned, no sign of turmoil in her face. "I'll also have dinner in my room, please, Henri. You may convey my regrets to Mr. O'Hara and my—Mr. von Hurst—if he should appear."

"Yes, madam, certainly. . . ."

She stripped off her clothing haphazardly in her room and immediately filled the large tiled tub in her bathroom with near-scorching bubbles. As she soaked she was gratified to feel tension ebb away, and warmth replace bitter cold. Her eyes were dry now, resigned and very tired. She had thought herself too upset ever to sleep again, but the opposite sensations were engulfing her. All she wanted to do was sleep.

She finally left the bath to dry herself with a large, snowy towel and slip into a floor-length burgundy silk caftan. Gretel appeared with her meal, a tender steak, which she surprisingly wolfed down. When she came to retrieve the tray, the slender housekeeper and cook glanced at her with concern.

"Mr. von Hurst and Mr. O'Hara both send their regards," Gretel said slowly, careful to pronounce the English she seldom used. "They instruct you to take care not to catch cold."

Ronnie gave Gretel a dry smile. "Mr. von Hurst went down to dinner tonight?"

"Yes, ma'am."

"Thank you, Gretel." Ronnie watched the middle-aged

woman leave her room and close the door before she chuckled. It was definitely a different night: the master had appeared and the mistress hadn't!

Her chuckle turned into a catch in her throat, and she curled onto the fur spread of her bed without removing the cover. Exhaustion took its toll, and as her mind continued to race with worry and pain her body gave up. She drifted into a sleep so deep that she wasn't plagued by a single dream.

The tapping on her door was light, so light that it was the persistence of the sound and not its echo that woke her.

She lifted her head, puzzled, groggy, and disoriented, then, alarmed as the noise continued, she hopped to her feet and flew to the door and threw it open.

Drake was standing in the dimly lit hall, as devastating as she had ever seen him. He had dressed for dinner in black velvet and white, an image of raw masculinity only semicivilized by nonchalant, but stunning, elegance.

Ronnie stared at him for a timeless second, unable to speak, enmeshed in the enigmatic, compelling demand of his dark eyes. Everything she had ever wanted stood towering in her doorway, motionless yet so very alive; arrogant and hard, yet strangely haunted and tender.

"I'm leaving in the morning," he told her, the assured timbre of his voice barely touched by a husky catch. "I came to say good-bye."

She had known the moment would come, but it caught her completely unaware. Her body congealed on her and she seemed detached from it, as if she had no control over limbs that felt like stone.

She finally forced a stiff nod, not trusting herself to speak.

"Oh, God, Ronnie!" he emitted in an explosive rasp. The door was pushed aside with a spontaneous shove, and Drake was in the room. She was enveloped into shaking arms that felt like bands of steel, and her cheek rested against the warm velvet texture of his jacket.

"Ronnie," he whispered, his hand stroking hair that was as silky as her caftan.

She looked up into his eyes. The vivid sapphire blue that met his gaze was clear but tremulous. Her lips were quivering, parted, sweetly moist.

He lowered his own to them, tenderly, lightly, reverently. He drew away, searching out her eyes, then the band of his arms tightened around her, and she was crushed to him, his kiss this time passionate, giving, taking, thirsting, bruising with intensity.

He would devour her.

Yet she met him with equal fervor, her fingers clinging to his broad shoulders, her nails digging into velvet. She noticed no pain as his lips consumed her, only the hunger and need that grew within both of them like wildfire. She accepted, she demanded in return, her tongue seeking his in a harmonious duel of longing that deepened with endless space. His fingers wound tightly through her hair, arching her neck, holding her for his driving demand in a grip from which she desired no escape. And when his mouth finally left hers, it moved tenderly down the exposed length of her throat, tasting, touching, flowering soft butterfly kisses.

He suddenly released her, only to lift her into his arms. Ronnie was delirious with him, drugged in the sensuality that was his tenderest touch as well as his passion. She was ready to forget everything. . . .

But she sensed a withdrawal from him as he laid her gently on the fur spread. Not the harsh withdrawal he had often displayed before, but a controlled, determined withdrawal that wrenched apart her heart and left it as torn and bleeding as his. Wild, passionate lovers, they were oddly, uniquely, moralists. It was Pieter's house.

He touched her forehead with his lips and moved away. For a moment longer he watched her, drinking in, absorbing, her beauty: the exquisite form molded by the silk caftan; the burnished sable hair softer, more lustrous, than the fur it was spread upon; the clear blue eyes, clearer than the sky, deeper than indigo; her face, delicate, regal, more finely sculpted than any piece of marble, ingrained with indomitable character.

The woman who had taught him the meaning of love, of loyalty and devotion.

He turned and left the room, a panther disappearing into the night.

Ronnie watched him go with a sense of emptiness that was overpowering. Her fingers moved shakily to her bruised lips, to the flesh still feeling the ravishment of his mustache and slightly rough cheeks.

She didn't cry—the pain was beyond that. And she didn't sleep again that night.

CHAPTER NINE

"I thought I'd never live to say it, Veronica, but you do look like hell."

Ronnie glanced up sharply from her third cup of coffee, praying the caffeine would put life in her veins.

Pieter looked surprisingly well.

She attempted a smile for him. "I thought I'd never live to say it," she retorted, "but you are a conniving, devious, and very, very wonderful man." She sobered. "But it's no good, Pieter. I'm going with you to Maryland."

He had been standing too long, even for the good health he was displaying. He took a chair beside her and tenderly touched a lock of her hair with a sigh. "I expected that you would fight me. You and Drake."

Ronnie closed her eyes, stricken afresh with a tug of war in her mind that was half guilt and love for Pieter, and half pain and love for Drake.

"Forgive me, Pieter," she murmured quietly. "I never meant to hurt you—"

"Veronica," Pieter interrupted, lifting her chin. "You are a priceless gem, so very rare, so very fine. I have nothing to forgive."

"Oh, Pieter, it wasn't right—"

"No!" he protested with a righteous vehemence that reminded her fleetingly of the great artist and man he had been before the illness had played havoc with his emotions and mind. "What wasn't right was us, Ronnie. Me in particular. The years you gave me, a sick old man clinging to a goodness and youth too devoted to do anything other than accept self-centered abuse. But no more, Ronnie. I will never throw you out of this, your home, and I will love you as my dear friend for the rest of my life and thank the gods for the time that you gave me. I will be delighted to take you to Maryland with me, as my very good friend, but we never will make our marriage legal. You and Drake are very right for each other, Ronnie. You will make him a marvelous wife."

She had thought herself cried out, but the encouragement, coming from the man she had betrayed, brought a flow of wetness down her cheeks. "Pieter . . ."

"There, there," he soothed, able to touch her now with his newly directed love. As husband and wife they were stilted strangers; as friends they could care with unstinting empathy. "Don't cry, Ronnie. Your future will bring all the happiness you have been denied. You must marry Drake."

"And what of you?" Ronnie charged through her tears.

"I am going to return to Paris," he told her, "for whatever time I do have. I am going to face the world. I am going to live as the great Pieter von Hurst!"

Ronnie smiled with sad admiration. "You are the very great Pieter von Hurst," she said softly.

"But first"—there was actually a twinkle in his pale blue gaze—"I shall attend your wedding. The papers will love it! We will tell them that we are divorced, of course. I will allow no scandal attached to your name!"

"Oh, Pieter!" Ronnie laughed. "You are the priceless one! I don't care about scandal, I care about your health. I care about—"

"Drake O'Hara." Ronnie flushed unhappily, and Pieter continued. "Please, Ronnie, no more sadness. You gave me all I could ever ask for—the spring of your life. But it's winter now for me, Ronnie, summer is left for you. A season for you to love."

"Pieter!" Ronnie protested. "I will not accept winter. And though you want now so much to give, you can't give me Drake.

He's gone. There are other things between us that can't be settled."

"He'll be back," Pieter said with conviction. He cleared his throat, and his next words took a great effort. "I have never held you in my arms, Ronnie, not as a man, but if I had, I know I would defy heaven and earth to hold you again."

Ronnie winced inwardly, flicking away the final trace of tears with her lashes. The immediate future was before them, and nothing would alter the course she planned to take.

"I think," she said, rising in a businesslike fashion, "that we'll have to discuss Paris and my future at a later date." She poured a fourth cup of coffee for herself and the first for Pieter, adding the heavy cream he liked. "We have a doctor to see first."

"Yes," Pieter said lightly. "We have a doctor to see." He drummed thin fingers on the table. "Ronnie?"

"Yes?"

"Whether the prognosis is good or bad, I am returning to Paris. Alone."

She nodded, her fingers trembling slightly as she set the coffee cups down. He reached out bony fingers to clasp her hand. "The prognosis may very well be good."

She nodded again, gulped her coffee down, mindless that she scalded her tongue, and left the dining room on a mumbled pretext of packing.

Pieter watched her, praying for her sake more than his own that the prognosis would indeed be good.

Four weeks later they were again sharing coffee, again talking as they had so belatedly learned to do.

But the dining table was different, the place was different, even the lifetime and dimension seemed to be different.

They were celebrating Pieter's forty-third birthday, and the celebration was a real one. Just that afternoon Ronnie had held his hand in hers as they waited for the verdict from a team of doctors. Their hands had been clammy together, but their expressions stoic. Only the two of them knew how their hearts beat with hope—a hope granted this time. The disease was still incurable, but new treatments could give Pieter an unknown lease on life. A life far easier. With new medication, his existence could be almost normal.

Now they sat in the coffee shop of their hotel, looking out of the veranda on the magnificent display of fall colors that were adorning Maryland in a natural beauty. It wasn't the peak of autumn yet, but the reds and golds of the trees had never seemed brighter, nor the grass greener.

And Ronnie was laughing. Pieter hadn't seen her laugh during the entire month. Her eyes, though, even as her lips curled, remained haunted. And he knew why, but he couldn't reassure her. He could only play God so far.

He reached a hand across the table and enveloped hers. "I would like it very much, Veronica," he told her, "if you would go upstairs and don your prettiest gown. An old and grateful man would like to take you to dinner."

"Old, never," Ronnie protested. Pieter now was ageless. He was still going to die, and he knew it, but as he pragmatically told Ronnie, they were all mortal, all subject to only so many years of life. He had been given many more and he intended to live each day to the fullest.

"Well, then, you must dress up for a very dear friend."

"I'll be glad to." She squeezed his hand back.

"Go on now," he persisted. "I shall call at your door in an hour."

Ronnie left him and returned to her room, which was actually a luxury suite. She wasn't really in a mood to dress elaborately for dinner—the last weeks had been filled with tension and strain during the day and fitful dreams of yearning and loss at night—but it was Pieter's birthday, and he was a new man, so like the kind and mature patron who had adopted her and Jamie all those years before.

She mechanically stripped off her tailored navy suit and adjusted the water for a shower. Beneath the steaming spray of heat and mist, she wondered what she would do. Pieter had given her

162

the island, but she didn't intend to return to it after he left. The house off Charleston could bring nothing but somber memories. She would have stayed with Pieter if he had wished it, but he was adamant, and determined that they split soon. Dependency, he informed her, was no life for either of them. He was putting all his affairs in order, and although he would have to return to Maryland several times a year, Paris was going to be his home. He had finished the marble series with her as his model before they had left, and he had given the press release that stated he and Ronnie were divorcing. It was wonderfully worded. She would always be "his dearest and most beloved friend."

Ronnie wondered as she listlessly showered if Pieter still imagined Drake would come back. She had dreamed of it at first, but as the days passed and no word was heard from him, she had to accept the truth.

Drake had gone home where life was normal, where women were in abundance, where he could forget his strange encounters and affairs on the remote, forbidding, windswept island. He hadn't even called to inquire about Pieter's health. He had entered her life with passion and a searing temper, and he was gone like a winter's thaw.

Leaving the shower, Ronnie surveyed her reflection with a grimace. She was terribly pale, and purple shadows were tinging beneath her eyes. She had to perk herself up; she would do nothing to ruin the wonderful night for Pieter.

After a careful application of makeup, she was more than satisfied. A brush of light blush had colored her cheeks; three-toned shadow and then mascara had subtly improved her eyes. A gloss of lipstick, and she could fool anyone, she promised herself.

On a whim she pulled the pins from her hair and brushed it loose. Another improvement. She could look almost young, almost gay, almost carefree. Pieter would love it.

She chose a dress of metallic blue that highlighted her eyes and complemented the waves of rich dark hair that cascaded over her shoulders. It was a daring dress for the one-time totally dignified

163

could wear such attire with such assured, raw masculinity. He was towering, beautiful, magnificent.

"Miss Flynn." He greeted her with a grave nod. "Are you ready?"

She wanted to throw her arms around him, to ignore everything but his presence, question nothing.

She chose fury instead. "Drake O'Hara. How nice to see you, except you're a little late, aren't you?" The weeks of loneliness, worry, and pain had driven her to the frenzy she felt now. "You've only come in time for the grand finale. Pieter has seen his doctors—the ones you arranged for—and he has already sweated through the diagnosis. It was good, thank you. He has finished his work. I'm afraid you left Chicago merely for a dinner."

Drake was laughing, pushing his way into the room.

"Stop it!" Ronnie hissed, fruitlessly pitting herself against his chest to prevent his entry. "You could have called, you could have written—"

"Damn!" he replied with amusement, catching her wrists to fend off her feeble pummeling. "To think I ever compared you to cold marble! You're as hot as volcanic fire—not that I don't love it!"

Ronnie stopped her assault with ired awe. "How dare you walk in here joking after—after—"

"Leaving when it was the only possible thing to do?" he supplied. He briskly led her to the carved love seat that dominated the salon of her suite. "Sit down, Miss Flynn."

"I will not—"

"Yes, you will." He smiled. "We've been through this before." Ronnie sat.

Drake pushed back his jacket to plant his hands upon his hips as he paced before her. "For your information, Miss Flynn, I have been in Maryland since the day you arrived. I have been in constant contact with Pieter."

Ronnie felt her jaw fall in a most undignified manner. He laughed and tapped it closed, then his expression sobered.

165

"I left when I did, Ronnie, because I knew you had to see this through with Pieter. I felt like a complete fool that day on the beach. You were right, I hadn't understood a thing. But dear God, Ronnie, I was in love with you, and I couldn't do a thing about it. How could I take you from a man like Von Hurst? I was continually frustrated, and I lashed out at you. I judged you because I couldn't bear the situation, and I had to have someone to blame. Then, when it appeared Pieter would do anything to be rid of you, you still didn't want me!"

He stopped his pacing and knelt on one knee before her, tenderly taking her hands in his. "I told you I was going to marry you, Ronnie. I meant it. I have Pieter's happy blessing, and nothing is going to stop me, not even you. I'll drug you and drag you down the aisle if I have to."

Moisture burned in Ronnie's eyes and she carried Drake's hands to her lips. "Oh, Drake! We still can't marry one another! You'll never trust me, and our lives would be a disaster."

Drake emitted an impatient oath, but Ronnie noted incredulously that it was directed at himself. "Ronnie, you have to forgive me for being an insufferable bastard. Trust you! I would trust you with my life—it's yours anyway—my heart, and my soul."

"But—"

"Ronnie," he interrupted, caressing her face with tender fingers and shaking it slightly as if he could force sense into her. "I believed at first that you and Pieter had had a very normal marriage, and that you had turned from him when he became ill—still caring, but not enough to endure a little chastity for the sake of his love and pride. I felt horrible when I entered his house and discovered I had had an affair with his wife. I admired the man, I respected him, I cared for him—and I had taken the one thing from him that a man doesn't take from another. I was furious with you, and I loathed myself, because even when I thought you were his wife, I wanted you still. I went through torture every night in that house. I wanted to run down the hall and ravish you—willing or no—in your husband's own home."

He stopped speaking abruptly and rose to sit beside her. His black eyes were on her with all the love and trust she could ever pray for. "I have to kiss you, Ronnie. I've gone crazy staying away this last month."

She did not protest as his lips touched hers with hungry reverence and his arms encircled her with firm possession. After a sweet infinity that threatened to grow dangerously passionate, he pulled away, gruffly explaining, "We are meeting Pieter for dinner."

"Oh, Drake," she choked, finally realizing the impact of what was happening through her reeling senses. "I can't believe this."

"I doubt if I'll ever stop being amazed at the sight and touch of you," Drake responded huskily. "You haven't said anything. Am I abducting you and dragging you down the aisle, or are you coming willingly?"

"Not willingly, eagerly." It was ridiculous; she wanted to run in wild circles, shouting for joy, but tears were streaking her cheeks.

Drake smoothed the dampness from her cheeks with the slightly rough touch of his thumbs. "What is it, Ronnie?" he demanded.

"Nothing, Drake," she assured him quickly, fingers trembling as they came to rest tentatively on the texture of his jacket. She laughed, wiping her own face with the back of her other hand. "I seem to cry so easily these days! But right now I'm happy, so happy. I never believed you wanted to spend your life with me. I thought you felt a proposal was the right thing to do—since you believed I'd be out in the cold. I wanted you to believe in me, forgive me, so badly, and I never thought it could happen."

"I was a pompous ass," Drake said baldly. "It is you who need to forgive me."

She thought of him, then, patiently waiting this month, on the sidelines all the time if needed, while she had carried out the commitment of her heart to another man. He had never left her, even when she sent him away. He had loved where she had loved,

167

given her a depth of comprehensive understanding that went beyond all speech and explanation.

"Drake," she cried suddenly, flinging herself onto his lap, mindless of her dress and his impeccable suit, to cling to his chest and bury her face in his neck, where the heady scent of his crisp and wild after-shave assailed her senses like a potent drug and sent delicious shivers to her spine. "I love you."

"I love you, sweet marble seductress," he hoarsely returned, cradling her to him and running a possessive hand down her spine. The shattering ferocity of his love took hold of him as he held her, his own now, his incredible creature of warmth, gentleness, and beauty, of quiet, stubborn pride and steadfast loyalty. His arms tightened around her. "No more tears, Ronnie. I'm going to make you happy, or die trying. We're going to do everything together, go everywhere together. We'll go anywhere you want. Rome, London, back to Paris. The honeymoon will be your choice. Where would you like to go?"

She raised eyes to him that now shimmered with crystal laughter. "Everywhere—eventually," she told him. "But for a honeymoon I want to take a cruise out of Charleston Harbor."

His own eyes twinkled and his mustache took on a lopsided twitch. "I'm crazy about cruises out of Charleston. I can guarantee you, I'm one man who will never knock southern hospitality —or charming southern belles." He planted a kiss on the tip of her nose. "Right now, we do have to get down to the lobby. Pieter is waiting."

"Drake." Ronnie paused with her fingers unnecessarily straightening his tie. "There's something else I'd like to do very much."

"And what is that?" He raised a querying brow.

"I want to go to Chicago." She raised impish eyes to his. "I want to meet your family, and all the little monster nephews and nieces. I want to meet the parents who could create such a creature as you!"

"I'm not sure how to take that, Miss Flynn," he replied with

168

mock severity. "You have to have respect for your future husband. I will be a man who insists upon you toeing the line!"

"As long as he toes it in return!" Ronnie said demurely.

"Oh, he will," Drake said airily, lacing his fingers through the hair at her nape. "But you, young lady, you keep in mind that he—your future husband—is a temperamental Irishman, prone to irate rages and use of a horsewhip on erring wives."

"I'll bear that in mind!" Ronnie promised gravely, ruining the effect entirely by bursting into a fit of giggles. She couldn't imagine Drake, who went into self-torture for control, horsewhipping anyone—not even a horse.

"Laugh at me, woman, would you?" he challenged sternly, adding a threatening "You will get yours."

Ronnie smiled mischievously and raised a doubting brow. "I guess we had better meet Pieter." His last statement, had she retorted, could have become very leading. They could have explored the potential meanings of his words for hours.

Pieter himself was magnificent in his own way that night. Slender and gaunt, he nevertheless made a handsome picture in his brocade jacket. Pride soared in Ronnie's heart for him, and she deserted an understanding Drake to slip her arm through Pieter's and plant a loving kiss upon his cheek.

His eyes were more alive that night than she had seen them in years. He smiled at her and squeezed her arm, but directed his comment to Drake. "You see, O'Hara, I told you she wasn't entirely unreasonable."

"I'm not quite convinced of that, Von Hurst," Drake replied, the curl of his lips obliterating his attempted frown. "But she has consented to marry me."

"Who needed my consent?" Ronnie charged with an indignant sniff, her chin tilting but her eyes sparkling. "It seems I'm the only one who hasn't known what's been going on. You two have obviously been conniving. I suppose I should consider myself lucky you brought me in on everything tonight!"

Drake met Pieter's eyes over her head. "Maybe we should feed her," he said innocently. "Is she always this cranky when hungry?"

"Hmmm . . ." Pieter replied absently. "Even when she isn't hungry. But dinner might cause an improvement. Let us go. I have a taxi waiting outside."

Dinner was Pieter's choice; it was his birthday, and a very real celebration of life. He had discovered a wonderful French restaurant near D.C. that he swore was "almost like dining on the Champs-Élysées."

He was right. The meal was authentically French, from the champagne to the delicate fruit dessert. The decor was intimate and pleasant, the room dimly lit, and a strolling violinist added just the right touch as he moved unobtrusively through the trellised vines that gave the lush wicker-and-velvet room a hint of the feel of a true terrace.

Drake and Pieter did most of the talking, and as she listened Ronnie marveled that her life could have held two such wonderful men, who both loved her deeply in their own special ways. Such a short time ago she could never have imagined such a scene, her relationship with Pieter turned to a binding friendship, her love for Drake turned to a commitment that would last forever. And Pieter and Drake, her two magnificent men, fast, sure friends.

It was a fairy-tale romance. She had her prince, but there were no evil warlocks. Only a magnanimous and benign king.

"Is that all right with you, Ronnie?"

"Pardon?" she realized guiltily that her mind had drifted from the conversation.

Drake smiled tolerantly. "You accuse us of not involving you," he complained teasingly, "but when we do, you don't pay any attention! Pieter and I were discussing the wedding taking place in three days. Pieter has made all the arrangements. It will be in the little chapel down the street from the hotel."

Ronnie's eyes flitted from Drake's to Pieter's. Pieter was grinning like a very smug Dutch cat. Ronnie felt tears coming to her eyes again, tears she couldn't dare show. Impulsively she jumped to her feet, threw her arms around Pieter's neck, and kissed both his cheeks.

A crimson blush filled his cheeks and he admonished her gruffly through the grin he couldn't force to fade. "Really, Veronica, such behavior is most undignified."

"Oh, I know!" she agreed with wide eyes. "Don't you just love it?"

"Yes," he mumbled into his demitasse cup, "yes, I do."

By the time Drake walked Ronnie back to her room that night, the future she had worried about had been settled. She and Drake would spend a few days in Chicago after the wedding, then fly back to Charleston to arrange for the transport of Pieter's marble sculptures. They were not going to be sold but dispersed to various museums. Von Hurst had taken his place with the masters.

As soon as Drake made the shipping arrangements Ronnie and he would leave for their honeymoon, and Pieter would shortly leave for his new life in Paris.

Henri and Gretel would be going with Pieter. Drake and Ronnie would take the horses and dogs. And Dave would care for the pleasure boats Drake kept on the Great Lakes.

Dreams could come true, Ronnie realized, her head spinning with the details the men conscientiously considered, with all ends tied up nicely.

Ronnie wasn't surprised when Drake followed her into the suite, but she was somewhat startled when he comfortably removed his jacket, vest, and tie and slung them casually over the arm of the love seat before seating himself to remove highly polished shoes.

He caught the consternation in her eyes and smiled with wicked amusement, answering her unvoiced question. "Yes, I am staying the night. This is not Pieter's house, and I can't stand one more minute of propriety. I'm not that much of a gentleman. And besides"—he moved toward her with slow deliberation, his feet soundless on the carpeted floor as he gapped the distance between them—"there is one thing I learned from Pieter that far surpasses any wisdom he gave me pertaining to sculpture." He took her face gently between his hands and looked deeply into her eyes. "Life is a very precious gift, not to be wasted. Love is even more precious. I am a very lucky man. I have them both. I don't intend to lose another second of either."

"Oh, Drake." Ronnie trembled as she circled her arms around his neck.

He smothered her against him, his hands raking the silklike hair down to her spine and beyond, to the two shadowed dimples he knew he would find at its base. "Ronnie," he groaned, the sound a thundering from deep within his chest. "You're crazy if you think I could leave you tonight. I haven't slept nights, dreaming of you the way I left you, your hair splayed across the fur, your provocative, beguiling shape so visible beneath that misty garment. In my dreams your eyes invited me, they were sparkling with liquid, sensuous beseechment. . . ."

She pulled away from him and asked wistfully, "Like they are now? Can the reality live up to the fantasy?"

"Reality," Drake said, pulling her back to his chest, where the beating of his heart combined with hers, "outshines the most fervent imagination in your case, my love." His kisses fell to the eyes that held such enchantment, they covered her face, and grazed the long slender column of her throat. A very familiar heat filled him, one only she could create, one only she could satisfy.

Ronnie felt as if her body melted to his like mercury. She could feel his rising desire, and her own spiraled to meet it. Her hips formed to his tauntingly while she arched to work at the buttons of his shirt. Her face tilted to his; her eyes became those of a cat, gleaming, exotically narrowed, seducing subtly with the hint of wild abandon. "Tell me more about your fantasies," she urged him, pulling his shirt from his waistband and allowing her fingers to provocatively run along the newly exposed flesh.

His satanic smile came into play as he caught her hands deftly and reversed the aggression, finding the zipper of her dress, releasing it, and allowing the fabric to fall to her feet like an ocean wave.

Indeed, he could well imagine she was Venus rising. Breasts of alabaster cream rose proudly over the lace of a teal-blue bra, her deep rose nipples peeking through the lace. He bent to remove the matching slip from her, allowing his hands to glide along her smooth midriff, over her hips, and down the velvet of her shapely legs as the slip too joined the dress on the floor. He heard her soft moan as his hands grasped her hips firmly, and his lips followed the course they had so recently taken. The sound of her pleasure sent his pulses racing to a fiery speed, and an urgent, fundamental, totally masculine, wildly primitive need to hold and conquer the exquisite feminine beauty that was his gripped him with shattering intensity. The dark depths of his passion showed in the taut lines of his face as he rose to meet his Venus, wordlessly sweeping her into his arms, leaving behind the discarded clothing as he swiftly walked her into the next room and lay her upon the bed. His eyes continued to hold hers as he impatiently doffed his clothes.

Ronnie watched him with unabashed longing, the warmth in her body growing as she anticipated the rough touch of the hair upon his chest against her breasts, which tingled and peaked in expectation. A quiver began to ripple through her. The extent of his desire was unmistakable, the sight of his long sinewed legs intoxicating.

His kisses ravaged her breasts as he hovered over her, even as he lifted her to him and sought the snaps to release the bra. Ronnie moaned and shuddered as he moved on to remove her last remaining garment, gossamer panties that slid sensuously down her legs. The heat in her was intensifying, but Drake found the core of her longing and stroked it languorously with knowing fingers that found in return complete reception. His eyes found hers again as he gave pleasure and sweet torment, and with a strangled cry she gripped her fingers in his hair to bring his face to hers. Her tongue traced the line of his mouth, then jutted into the demanding warmth. She felt as if she were going mad with

173

her own desire, whirling into endless space with a burst of sensation. Her mouth left his to bite lightly into a bronze shoulder, her body undulating to his, speaking a plea of its own as she beseeched him with barely comprehensible whispers to make her his.

"Fantasy, my love, or reality?" he whispered hoarsely.

"A little bit of both," she sighed. "Drake . . ."

He moved from her for a brief moment, one well used. His kisses covered her body moistly, feverishly, seeking all the places his hands had discovered and reawakening them even further into a flame run so rampant, it threatened to consume her. Each of Ronnie's pleasure-filled responses drove Drake to heightened desire, and he lowered himself over her, spreading thighs that wound to his own sinewed ones with the sweetest of welcomes.

"Forever, Ronnie," he groaned, shuddering fiercely with the wonderful release of taking her, becoming one with her in a volatile entry. "All this forever, my love."

Her answer was a moan, inaudible, but heard by him. "Forever." It was forever. Stroking, gliding, sailing into the stars. Drake's passion and desire were such that he was rough, but his aching love guided even that ardor, and he took her with him every step of the way. Their rhythm was mutually combustible, wild as the wind they both adored, as natural and primitive as the inevitable predestiny that had brought them together as man and woman.

The tempo increased, madly, sweetly, aided and abetted by the fact that neither could keep their hands still. Their lips would cling and part, their tongues touch, duel. The end, the beginning of heavenly oblivion, came upon them together as a crescendo of tenderly violent impact that left them both in trembling awe, satiated, saturated with wonder. They did not part but held tight together, waiting in languorous pleasure for their breath to return and the quivering of their limbs to subside.

The satisfaction of their union, tenfold sweet with the admission of a binding love, had exhausted Ronnie. Her eyes began to close in a rest that was overwhelming with the release of all the tensions she had suffered—pain, worry, denial. She had cast them all upon Drake's broad shoulders, and in the wild and chaotic beauty of their union she had found peace.

She blinked, realizing she had dozed off, to find Drake seated Indian-style on the bed, drawing idle patterns around her navel. A very slow smile crept into her lips as she watched him through lazy, half-closed eyes. A smug thrill of feminine satisfaction invaded her; there was something boyish about his pose as he sat vulnerably naked, yet there was nothing boyish about his sinewed physique, taut over his bone structure even as he leaned forward.

He knew intuitively that she had wakened, asking without glancing at her face, "Are you happy, Ronnie?"

She nodded and caught the hand caressing her skin to kiss it. "So happy, and scared. Can this really last?"

His strongly planed features grew grave. "Yes, it can. Not every minute can be ecstasy, or blind passion, but love can be—and ours will be—a shelter against outside storms. Love is trust, and peace and security in that trust. It's a wonderful thing, even in the worst of times."

Ronnie absorbed his words without speaking, her eyes downcast. When she opened them, she found Drake watching her with a brooding intensity.

"Why didn't you tell me that you'd never made love to Pieter?"

She caught her breath and watched him blankly for a second. "How did you know?"

"He told me."

Ronnie gasped with surprise. Her voice quavered. "When?"

"We had quite an interesting dinner that last night. Pieter told me a lot I already knew—about Jamie's death and your marriage in Paris. He also told me a lot you didn't. He told me that you knew from the very beginning that you were entering a platonic marriage." Drake paused for a minute. "He also told me how bad it was for you all those years, how he used and abused you, and how you withstood it all with unbreakable patience and endurance."

Ronnie's hand tightened convulsively on the one she held. Her lashes lowered and she held her voice steady. "It wasn't that bad, Drake. You see, I always knew the real Pieter von Hurst. I knew he would never really hurt me. I knew that no one else could understand what he went through as I did. I—" She stuttered momentarily. "I never told you that our marriage had always been platonic because one thing Pieter clung to was his pride."

Drake adjusted his weight over hers and gently took her chin in his hands. "Look at me, Ronnie," he commanded with tenderness. "I'm not angry or upset that you didn't tell me. I admire what you tried to do. All these wonderful quirks of that crazy proud personality of yours are what make me love you so very much."

Her heart was in her eyes as she met his, offering the depths of a soul that had remained innocent and pure through everything.

"Oh, Drake," she murmured with loving gratitude, placing kisses of tremulous emotion in the hollows of his collarbone. "And I love you so much for all that you are!" Her voice softened. "For all that you've done for Pieter."

Drake smiled at her. "I have to admit, it's been a lot easier to be Pieter's friend now that I know you two were never lovers. You can't imagine what it's like to sit at a dinner table with a man and try to carry on a normal conversation when you know you've made love to his wife."

Ronnie chuckled and sobered. "Drake—you know I'll always be concerned for him."

"Yes, Ronnie," he said gently. "I do know. And I'll always share that concern with you."

He shifted back to a sitting position abruptly, pulling her with him into his arms. "Enough of this deep conversation for the night!" he charged severely. "If one of us slips on a robe, I think we might find a bottle of champagne chilling outside the door to the suite."

"Champagne?" Ronnie arched a brow with amusement. "Mr. O'Hara, you do know how to treat a fiancée!"

"Of course." Drake grinned, lifting her slightly to give her underside a light swat. "And since I thought of the champagne—French, of course—I think you should run out and get it."

Giggling, Ronnie jumped from the bed. "This time, O'Hara. But don't get any ideas that I'll always jump when you swat!"

Drake laced his hands behind his head and made himself comfortable on the pillow while Ronnie grabbed a robe. "Hurry!" he ordered imperiously, ignoring her comment. "By the way—I hope you had a lot of sleep last night, because I don't want you to count on much tonight."

"Promises, promises!" Ronnie said mockingly, sighing.

Drake threw a pillow at her but missed. He grinned fully, his face a devil's mask.

"I always keep my promises."

CHAPTER TEN

They were married as planned three days later.

Pieter von Hurst did attend the wedding. The papers, of course, got hold of the story, but the three involved found outside perplexity over the situation nothing more than amusing.

Drake and Ronnie then flew to Chicago, where she met his parents. They were a charming couple, accepting her immediately with open arms. Drake's mother, an incredibly tiny woman to have produced such a son, was an attractive and spirited lady, literally pooh-poohing any fears Ronnie might have had about her being concerned with Ronnie's notoriety.

The senior O'Hara was a Gaelic charmer, and Ronnie could easily see where Drake had inherited his size, coloring, and dangerously charismatic eyes. His speech enchanted Ronnie; he still carried the lilt of a brogue after almost forty years in the States.

Drake watched with tolerant amusement as his parents and Ronnie instantly endeared themselves to one another. He had expected nothing less, and he thanked God fervently for both his mother and father when he saw the happiness in his bride's eyes that night. "Oh, Drake," she told him wonderously, "not only do I have you, but a family, too! It's been so long. . . ."

He chuckled and enveloped her in his arms tenderly. She was so terribly strong, yet so sweetly vulnerable. "You definitely have a family," he replied ruefully. "They've adopted you already. In fact, I think they prefer their new daughter to their son!"

They weren't able to see much of Chicago, as Drake had spent too much time away from work and had to put some time in at the main gallery. Ronnie didn't care. She assured Drake that the city wasn't going to go away, and spent her days between her in-laws' house and her own new home.

Drake's house was like the man—tasteful, fastidious, yet very warm and masculine. It was a split-level modern house done in brick and wood that complemented both the manicured lawn and rock garden and the untouched woodland that stretched behind it. A terrace of three-sided glass looked upon the rock garden, and Ronnie found herself continually drawn to the spot, trying to convince herself that the magical place was really her new home.

"Like it?" Drake asked, slipping his arms around her waist and resting his chin on her head.

"Love it," Ronnie replied, slipping her hands over the pair that held her.

She ran her eyes over the room. Drake's love for art was apparent everywhere: exquisite sculptures adorned the tables, paintings decked the walls with clever display. A strong macrame swing extended from a brass fitting in the corner of the room like an intricately woven birdcage. Earth tone throw pillows were nestled into the seat, and Ronnie blissfully imagined hours of curling into its circumference with a good book, swinging lightly, looking up now and then to view the garden through the spotless glass.

"Change anything you want," Drake directed with a smile. "Hell—find a new house if you want! I am fond of this place, though. We have five acres, and we're still only a thirty-minute drive from the heart of the city."

"I love the house," Ronnie assured him, "and I don't want to change a thing. Except maybe the—"

"The what?"

"The bedroom." Ronnie grimaced ruefully. "Not that I don't like it"—she thought of the room with its high platform bed, polished oak bookshelves and dressers, and rich chocolate drapes and bedspread—"it's just a little too male!" She smiled slowly at his confusion. "I want anyone who walks into that room to know that you do share it with a wife!"

Drake laughed, but while he was gone that afternoon a package arrived for her. It was a huge luxurious white alpaca spread. Drake hadn't signed his name, just the word *fantasy*.

Ronnie laughed delightedly and quickly changed the spread. It made a wonderful change, coupled with the feminine articles she now had resting on her dresser, it made the room very intimate, very much that of a couple. White drapes, she decided, would be the finishing touch. But they could come later. . . .

When Drake returned home, his fantasy was fulfilled. She waited for him, swathed in the sheerest of black negligees, stretched languorously on the fur, her hair a startling contrast of thick sable waves. Her eyes were those he had always imagined, captivating, seductive, heavy with a passion uniquely for him. . . . She was his marble beauty, half kitten, half tigress.

Later, when their bodies had cooled and they clung together beneath the fur for warmth, Drake tugged lightly at a strand of silky hair tangled in his fingers. His eyes were deeply brooding as Ronnie stared into them.

"Do you miss Von Hurst?" he asked softly.

"No," she answered with honesty, meeting his gaze before issuing light kisses on each corner of his mustache. "I went days without ever seeing Pieter when I lived on the island, and . . ."

"And what?" Drake persisted, willing his mind off the lips that were stirring his senses again.

She flushed lightly and buried her head in the black curls on his chest. "When I'm in your arms," she muffled softly to him, "I don't miss anything. I don't even remember that there is an outside world. . . ."

He stroked her hair, the contours of her back, and marveled at the wonderful combination of modesty and passion that was his wife. He had asked the question because they were returning to the island tomorrow. She had told the truth, and yet he still worried slightly. She had been away from the man she had cared for only a week, and she knew she would see him again. Her loyalty was deep, not easily broken. Would seeing him again tear her apart all over? There would be a finality to the break up of the barren island off Charleston's coast. . . .

He thought no more. Like her, he forgot there was an outside world when they came together in one another's arms.

The next days were grueling. Though Von Hurst appeared fit, and pleased to see them in an admirably friendly fashion, he could take little part in the work ahead. Hired labor took care of the transfer of animals and furniture, but as artists, neither Drake nor Pieter would trust the packing of the marble pieces to anyone else. Ronnie learned in those days that her new husband had a streak of perfectionism that was amazing. At least, she thought with dry tolerance as she repacked a box for the third time, he had the will and strength to ask no more than he gave.

He looked up suddenly from the pile of insulating material he separated with his strong, sure hands and laughed.

Ronnie sent him a querying frown.

"You'll never be able to accuse me of chauvinism." He chuckled to her dryly. "How many men would allow their wives' backs to be on display in museums all over the world?"

"The back is attached to a head," Ronnie retorted.

"And a derriere," Drake reminded her sternly.

She watched him for a moment, wondering if there were just the hint of a curl to his lips. "*Do* you mind?" she asked him.

He crawled through the various debris on the floor and held her, one hand molding over the anatomy under discussion. "No," he said, and there was a decided curl to his lips. "Not when I was in on the creation. But I do think the world has seen the end of the modeling career of Mrs. Drake O'Hara. If you get any professional urges, you'll have to come to me."

"You are a chauvinist," Ronnie informed him.

"Do *you* mind?"

She shook her head with mischief in her eyes. "Not at all. I can handle you."

Drake was undaunted. "That's right," he said gravely, fingering the band he had recently placed on her finger. "You can handle me whenever you like."

He teased her through all the work they did, and even when Pieter was present, the mood remained light. Meals were pleasant affairs with conversation running smoothly. But as the inevitable time to leave drew near, Drake knew that Ronnie was straining to remain cheerful.

The hour of their departure came. Ronnie was as beautiful and elite as ever, her apparel a smart beige suit with a vest that emphasized her slender curves beneath the tailored jacket. She wore shoes and a hat of complementing tan, and Drake thought with an admiring amusement that Ronnie was a clotheshorse. She had an instinctive ability to choose clothing, and each accessory was always perfect. Her hat dipped low over one eye, and he was reminded of the first time he saw her. She would always be innately regal, mysterious and intriguing. And always wear her pride like her clothing, a valiant shield that was impenetrable. Except to him. He concealed a tender smile, suddenly completely secure.

"Go say good-bye to Pieter," he told her.

"Alone?"

"Yes, I'll carry the bags and meet you at the boat."

Ronnie tapped at the door to Pieter's suite for the last time. She smiled and bit her lip as she heard his imperiously clipped, *"Entre!"*

She opened the door and found him by the window, looking out, his thin hands clasped behind his back. His light eyes turned to her, and a soft smile curved into delicate lips.

"Everything is ready!" she began cheerfully. Then the effort failed. Her lips quivered and her eyes started to fill. "We're leaving."

His arms extended to her as they never could have before. She rushed to him, and the tears fell as he held her.

182

"Don't cry for me, Ronnie. Please, don't cry." He wiped the tears from her cheeks. "You gave me my art; you gave me life when I desired to end it. You must give me one more thing."

"What is that?" she asked, trying to smile again as she wiped her own eyes.

"The promise that you will live long and happily, and take all that Drake can give you."

Ronnie nodded, fearful that if she tried to speak, the tears would fall again.

"I haven't lost a wife, you know," he told her, pale blue eyes searching hers. "A man cannot lose what was never rightfully his. I have, instead, gained a friend, and a very talented protégé to boot."

Ronnie nodded again, the shimmering beauty of her eyes giving him a love he would cherish to his dying day.

He kissed her forehead and shoved her lightly for the door. "Go now, Veronica. And don't cry. You will see me again."

She walked to the door with her head bowed, pausing before she whispered, "Take care of yourself, Pieter."

"You too, Ronnie."

She swung around like a water sprite and flew back to him with a strangled cry. He held her for second, and pushed her away. "Stop it, Ronnie," he said gruffly. "You're getting tears all over my shirt, and it's silk. Go now and tell that protégé of mine that he'd better take care of you and make you happy."

Ronnie fled the room. Perhaps she had given Pieter his life, but he had also given her hers. He had given her Drake.

She moved swiftly out of the house, and in the garden that had once been her sanctuary, she reconciled all that her life had been with all that her life would be. Plucking a single rose, she held it to her cheek, then slowly left the garden and walked the pathway to the dock.

Her footsteps quickened as she neared the boat. Drake was already there, patiently waiting, his tall dark form a towering bastion of strength. He reached out a bronze hand and took hers, enveloping it with warmth and a tender, secure pressure.

183

A promise to love and share into eternity was in the grip of that bronze hand, and as it led her onward Ronnie knew she would always follow without looking back, loving and trusting in return.

Statuesque. She was still a marble beauty, but like the exquisite marble work of the masters, she was alive, warm, vibrant, and bewitching.

She watched him, and he knew it; he returned her appreciative gaze.

They had had enough sun; it was time to fulfill the messages of their eyes.

He executed a perfect dive into the pool, and so did she.

His touch upon her satiny skin in the water was sheer agony to nerves heightened with anticipation. His breath, as he whispered in her ear, was a stimulant that sent her senses reeling. "I'm Drake O'Hara, madam, and don't you ever forget it. I'd like to buy you a drink, but not poolside—in *our* cabin."

"That's nice," she murmured in return, nibbling at his lower ear and feigning a mock defiance, "then I can buy you one—in *our* cabin."

"If you don't stop that," Drake warned, pressing against her so that she gasped with the evidence of his desire, "we won't make it out of the pool."

Laughing, they broke apart, but they were scarcely through the cabin door before Drake pulled the string of her bikini top, robbing her of the garment as she glided ahead of him. Uttering a startled chastisement, Ronnie swung around to him.

She was a golden-tanned, exquisite, perfectly molded, proud beauty, the breasts he had bared high and firm, her waist a wraithlike thing of satin that led to lusciously carved hips. Her chin was tilted in mock query and indignation for only a second, and then she was in his arms, her soft breasts crushed to his hair-roughened chest, sensitively hardened nipples teasing and teased by the crisp depth of black curls.

"Ronnie," he whispered with a groan that rippled a shudder through his torso. He caught her head and looked deeply into the pools of sapphire that had long ago bewitched him, and then he kissed her, softly at first, then deeply with an exploding passion, seeking every sweet crevice of her mouth with a plundering tongue. She returned his play with a fire of her own, moaning as their bodies meshed together with heat, taunting him further with gentle nips upon his lower lip to be followed by the tantalizing and healing balm of the moistly tender tip of her tongue. It was she who pulled away to search out his eyes and demand with panted breath, "What do you want, Drake?"

He grinned but his eyes held warning. "I want you," he growled, scooping her into his arms with a steellike force that advised her there would be no more teasing. "Now, and forever."

"Sir," she returned meekly, "you have got me—now and forever."

She was aflame for him as he deposited her upon the bed, impatiently divesting her of the bikini bottom, and exploding with incoherent murmurs of desire as he planted kisses into the newly exposed hollows of her hips. She began to quiver uncontrollably, and he continued his assault almost savagely, claiming her flesh with moist, heated lips from the tender rise of her breasts to the invitation of her sleek thighs, alternately demanding fiercely and grazing with the utmost reverence.

Ronnie's fingers clutched feverishly into the thick black luster of Drake's hair, trying to bring him to her before the longing he had elicited drove her wild. "Drake!" she pleaded desperately, moaning delightedly with each intimate assault. "Oh, Drake. . . ."

His weight moved firmly over hers, pinioning her with the incredibly toned form that enveloped her into another, permeating world of sheer mindless delight. His heated flesh quivering like hers seemed to combine them in endless time and space. But though he pulsed against her and teased with taunting proximity, he again gripped her face firmly between his hands and gratingly countered, "What do you want, Ronnie?"

"You," she whispered, searching his eyes.

"Forever?" he queried, then touched her lips. "It isn't just a word."

"Forever," she vowed gravely. "Oh, God, Drake, no, it isn't just a word. Forever and ever and ever. . . ."

Her answer satisfied his mind, her movements satisfied his body. He had loved her from the beginning, but now that love was his, rightfully his, and the emotion guided their lovemaking. Their coupling was passionately wild, abandoned as the sea, as deep and obliterating as the sizzling dark depths of his eyes. But it was more than that. The intimate rhythm that drove them to the highest peaks of ecstasy was that of a combining of two perfectly attuned bodies; it was also the consummation of two minds that worked as one, two souls in harmony, two hearts that gave endlessly, unabashed to take in return. . . .

They crested upon that pinnacle of sheer ecstasy together, their release so volatile, it almost stole consciousness, leaving them to shudder delightfully in one another's arms as they left their solely private dimension to travel together back to solid earth. Drake was loathe to move from her, even as he relaxed with the sense of fulfillment. He was a part of her, physically for the time, and it was right, it felt wonderful. He would stay where he was, savoring his love.

She opened sapphire eyes and stared into his with a tender smile. She understood, she felt the same. Dusk began to fall as they lay contentedly together.

Later, comfortably situated, Ronnie's burnished sable head resting in the tender embrace of her husband's shoulder, they began to talk, to laugh, to plan their lives. Funny, though, they didn't really need to speak to communicate. Their silences were always companionable.

It was during one of those silences that Ronnie realized the vision of dark eyes would always impose upon any other. She would never forget the pale blue—she didn't want to. But those wonderful dark eyes that had haunted her from first sight would beguile her for eternity with love, with tenderness, with the understanding that would last even beyond youth and passion. . . .

Drake adjusted his length, as always, sensing her moods.

Dark-brown eyes stared into hers even as she envisioned them, gentle with the understanding she cherished.

"I love you," he said softly. It was all that was necessary.

"Forever," she returned with a smile.

His lips descended upon hers with gentle, overwhelming command, and there was no past. Only a glittering future of love . . . together, forever.

COMING
IN
AUGUST—

NEW DELL

TEMPESTUOUS EDEN,
by Heather Graham.
$2.50

Blair Morgan—daughter of a powerful man, widow of a famous senator—sacrifices a world of wealth to work among the needy in the Central American jungle and meets Craig Taylor, a man she can deny nothing.

EMERALD FIRE,
by Barbara Andrews
$2.50

She was stranded on a deserted island with a handsome millionaire—what more could Kelly want? Love.

NEW DELL

LOVERS AND PRETENDERS,
by Prudence Martin
$2.50

Christine and Paul—looking for new lives on a cross-country jaunt, were bound by lies and a passion that grew more dangerously honest with each passing day. Would the truth destroy their love?

WARMED BY THE FIRE,
by Donna Kimel Vitek
$2.50

When malicious gossip forces Juliet to switch jobs from one television network to another, she swears an office romance will never threaten her career again—until she meets superstar anchorman Marc Tyner.